Welcome to the wonderful wo
For a free short story and to listen to me read the first chapter of all my other Regencies, please go to my website:

https://romancenovelsbyglrobinson.com

Thank you!

GL Robinson

The Lord and The Bluestocking

A Regency Romance

By

GL Robinson

©GL Robinson 2021. All Rights Reserved.

As always, in memory of my dear sister, Francine.

With thanks to my Beta readers, who always tell me what they think.

And with special thanks to CS, for his patient editing and technical help and more especially, his friendship.

Cover art: GL Robinson, 2023

Contents

Chapter One 1
Chapter Two 5
Chapter Three 13
Chapter Four 19
Chapter Five 27
Chapter Six 31
Chapter Seven 39
Chapter Eight 45
Chapter Nine 49
Chapter Ten 53
Chapter Eleven 59
Chapter Twelve 63
Chapter Thirteen 71
Chapter Fourteen 75
Chapter Fifteen 83
Chapter Sixteen 89
Chapter Seventeen 93
Chapter Eighteen 99
Chapter Nineteen 103
Chapter Twenty 109
Chapter Twenty-One 115
Chapter Twenty-Two 123
Chapter Twenty Three 129

Chapter Twenty-Four 137
Chapter Twenty-Five 143
Chapter Twenty-Six 149
Chapter Twenty-Seven 153
Chapter Twenty-Eight 159
Chapter Twenty-Nine 165
Chapter Thirty 169
Chapter Thirty-One 177
Chapter Thirty-Two 183
Chapter Thirty-Three 189
Chapter Thirty-Four 193
Epilogue 197
Excerpt from the best-selling Regency novel: A Marriage is Arranged 201
Note from the Author 206
Regency Novels by GL Robinson 207
About The Author 211

Chapter One

Passing the reading desk to search in the high bookshelves beyond, Lord James Farrell beheld a sight that to any other man would have been distinctly pleasurable. A nicely rounded female rump was presented to his view, the head and shoulders of its owner apparently engaged in a search for something in one of the lower drawers inset into the reading desk. However, Lord James's mind was dwelling on a report he had read that morning. It said that the size of a mature cow reared under the improved grazing conditions had increased from an average of 370 pounds in the last century to 840 pounds achievable nowadays. The rump presented to him thus merely caused him to wonder what the rear end of an 840 pound heifer must look like, and the delights of the scene were consequently lost on him.

It was not the only sight lost on him. He was in London's most celebrated bookshop, *The Temple of the Muses*. It was a gloriously lofty place, with high bookshelves on three sides and a circular reading desk in the center. Above it soared the interior of a cupola that gave credibility to its name. He noticed none of that, either.

He had come in search of anything that might have been written by Robert Bakewell. This agriculturalist had died some twenty years earlier, having become world famous with his sheep and cattle breeding program. His lordship knew it had all begun with improving the grazing through the irrigation and fertilization of pasturelands. He had plans for the Farrell lands and wanted to learn more about it. He could have visited the Norfolk estate of Thomas Coke, Bakewell's acolyte, but hated the idea of listening to the man's endless pontificating. So here he was.

As he approached, the owner of the rump must have heard his footfall, for a head emerged from the drawer and a flushed countenance looked up at him.

"Oh!" said the young woman thus discovered, "I'm sorry. Am I in the way?"

"What?" Farrell was brought to earth with a thump. "What did you say?"

"I thought I might be in your way."

"Er...," his lordship was confused. Why should this young woman think she was in his way? He was heading to the bookshelves. She was looking in the drawer, wasn't she? What had one to do with the other?

"No," he said finally.

"Oh, good." She was silent for a moment then looked up at him again. "You don't happen to know anything about the flora and fauna of the Tahitian Islands?" she asked earnestly. "I can't find any pictures at all."

She gazed at him again and Lord Farrell looked at her intently. That was not, it must be said, because he found her attractive, but because he was thinking if he knew the answer to her question. In fact she was nothing extraordinary *au fait de beauté,* as her tonnish aunt would have said, with her brown hair braided under a serviceable bonnet and rather ordinary blue eyes. But she had a vivacity of expression that most people found attractive, and she was generally held to be a well-looking young lady.

For her part, she saw he was above average height and handsome in a square-jawed kind of way. But his eyes were so dark as to be almost black and his stare was disconcerting. His very dark hair looked as if it needed a cut and the rest of him was not much better. His shirt collar was wilted and his neckcloth showed evidence of having been pulled at in irritation. The cuffs that showed beneath his coat were not very clean. He wore scuffed top boots, surely unsuitable for town wear, and his coat certainly had not needed the services of two men to ease him into it. He must have shrugged it on anyhow, and it hung down his sides, weighted by obviously full pockets. He was still staring at her.

"The thing is," she explained, "I want my illustrations to look realistic."

Since he gave no response, she went on, "I intend to write and illustrate children's books, you see. Not the improving tales I remember thinking so boring and stupid when I was a girl. I mean, were children ever so good and kind as the ones in some of them, or taught anything by the horrible tortures inflicted on them for bad behavior in others? Why can't children be taught real things about the world around them? Things that actually happen. Wouldn't you much rather your children learn about those?"

Lord Farrell was by now thoroughly alarmed. He had still been thinking about the answer to her first question when she threw more at him. He had no idea what this young woman was talking about. His children? He had no children. He'd never considered having any. He'd have to be married for that, and that was something he most definitely did not want.

"Er... no," he said desperately.

"No?" She seemed shocked. "You'd rather they read all that old stuff?"

"Look, Miss... er..."

"Maxwell. Elisabeth Maxwell, though I'm usually called Ellie."

"Miss Maxwell, I've no idea what you are talking about. I have no knowledge at all of Polynesia and I know nothing about children or what they read. I've come to look for material about improving cattle grazing—in England," he added, as if she might imagine he was talking about the South Seas.

"Oh." She digested that information. "Well, did you enjoy stories like Little Goody Two Shoes when you were little? Or about Timmy who was eaten by a giant because he disobeyed his mother?"

In fact, his lordship could remember reading such stuff as a child and he had thought it all very silly.

"No. I didn't like it at all."

He seemed to have said the right thing, for Miss Maxwell exclaimed, "Exactly! That's why I want to write about and illustrate places and things children can either see around them or aspire to see when they're older. I've decided to begin with de Bougainville's voyage to the Tahitian islands but I need more illustrations."

There was a silence. James could think of nothing to say, and Ellie realized she had indulged her worst flaw: talking too much.

"Well," she said at last, "I've kept you too long, Mr....?" she held out her hand.

"Er... Farrell,' said his lordship. "James Farrell."

He took her hand and seemed about to shake it, then some remembered lesson must have come to him, for he bowed over it instead.

"At your service," he mumbled.

He hesitated a moment, then gave a brief nod, and walked away. He did not look back.

Chapter Two

Having been singularly unlucky in finding anything written by Robert Bakewell, James Farrell left *The Temple Of The Muses* none the wiser. He had paid no more attention to Miss Maxwell. In fact, intent on his own mission, he had forgotten her existence the minute he left her.

He walked home to Farrell House, so deep in thought that he did not see a number of his acquaintances attempt to catch his attention as they rode by. But since they had mostly been boys together both at Eton and at Oxford, they knew him well. It was impossible to talk to him when he was in a study, so no one took it amiss or thought any the worse of him.

He was an odd duck, they all knew. Not a bad fellow and would give you his last shilling. Not that it would be possible for him to be reduced to such penury, his father being one of the warmest men in London. Rich enough to buy an abbey. Old Jim would inherit the lot, lucky devil. What he would spend it on, only the Lord knew. He never bought himself a new coat unless his valet went on his knees to beg him, and he had never been known to encourage any of the fair Cythereans who from time to time tried to break through his distracted demeanor.

If he ever went to a Ball, he had to be reminded to sign his name on one or two of the dance cards dangling from the wrists of hopeful maidens. Then he had to be reminded to actually dance when the time came. Once on the floor, he generally acquitted himself quite well, so long as someone told him what he was supposed to be dancing. For some reason, he had a prodigious memory for dance figures. Someone once asked him how he remembered all the steps when he forgot who he was supposed to be performing them with. "It's just mathematics," he had answered seriously. "I never forget those patterns either."

Having him as your neighbor at the dinner table was a trial. He would stare at you and answer the most simple question as if it were a matter of the utmost seriousness. When asked whether he was enjoying the fine weather presently smiling upon the capital, he had been known to expound upon the meteorological events that were producing it. When one hostess asked him with a smile whether he was particularly enjoying the lamb cutlets he was devouring at great speed, he answered, "Oh, is that what it is? I hadn't noticed. I'm very hungry. I don't think I ate at all today."

Hostesses of the *ton* nevertheless continued to invite him. While he was often beside the point and disconcerting with his intent stare, he was kind, his rare smile was charming, and... well, his family was so very wealthy.

Arriving at Farrell House, Lord James entered the front hall to the news his father was in his study and had been asking for him.

"'Pon my word, James," declared the Marquess when he saw him. "I never saw such an ill-fitting coat in my life. And for heaven's sake arrange your neckcloth. It's all anyhow. And what in God's name have you in your pockets? The sides of your coat are weighed down as if by anchors. I'm amazed Furber let you leave the house like that."

His son fumbled vaguely with his neckcloth, making no appreciable difference to it, then looked down at his pockets. He plunged his hands in and drew forth a coiled metal ruler, a bound-up length of string, four iron stakes, a penknife, a very dirty handkerchief, a pile of coins and a leather-covered notebook with a stubby pencil in its folds.

"Oh," he said. "I wondered what had happened to that ruler." He unwound it and let it spring back into its coil.

"I am at a loss to know why you should carry any of that paraphernalia with you through the streets of London," said his father, with exasperation. "A *clean* handkerchief, a few coins and, at the limit, a penknife is all that a gentleman should require. You may keep your notebook and your banknotes in your breast pocket, like a gentleman."

"Is that what you wanted to see me about, father? The contents of my pockets?"

"Of course not!"

His father seemed on the verge of losing his temper, but remembering previous similar encounters with his son in which he had never managed to make his point, controlled himself.

"I only ask you to try to appear more like the scion of a fine old family and less like a land surveyor," he said. Then, with a further attempt at calmness, "Look, my son, the future of this family depends on you. I shall not live forever and neither will you. You are what, nearly thirty years old? You are in your prime and should be setting up your nursery. You must have a son to continue the family line. You know if you don't, it'll all go to your damned cousin Eustace. So far, the silly fool has only produced a daughter, but I hear his wife is increasing again. Let's hope it's a boy this time, or the line is in danger of dying out entirely."

"That's interesting," replied his son, ignoring the last half of his father's complaint. "You are the second person today who has talked about my children. She wanted to know what they read."

"*She*? Who is this *She*?" His father leaped up from behind his desk. "Can I hope—a young woman? Have you met someone at last with whom you have actually discussed *children*? Who is she? Who's her father?"

"Father, I simply cannot answer all your questions if you hurl so many at me at once. Yes, she is a young woman, no we have not discussed children except in as far as what they might usefully read. Her name is… is… let me see, yes, her name is Elisabeth Maxwell, and I've no idea who her father is, or if she even has one."

"Of course she has a father! Everyone has one!"

"Now, you know, father, that's not strictly true. Pompey Smith's father died last year, so he hasn't got one, and…"

"Don't be ridiculous! You know what I mean! What is her family? Is she the daughter of a gentleman? She's not an opera dancer, I hope? Though I've never heard of you being interested in women of that type—indeed in any women at all, God help us."

"Again, father, allow me to answer one question before you ask another. I know nothing of her family, but yes, I judge her to be a lady, not an opera dancer. At least, she never mentioned it. She said she was a writer, or wanted to be a writer—of children's books."

"A writer? She's not a bluestocking, is she?" The Marquess looked worried.

And as his son began to answer, he hastened on. "Never mind, never mind! So long as she's a gentlewoman, healthy and capable of bearing strong sons, she can be as bluestockinged as she likes! Now, where is she, and when can I meet her? I'll send a note tomorrow to see when St. George's is available for a wedding. We shouldn't waste time. Oh, blessed day! If only your dear mama were here to see it."

The Marquess took a snowy handkerchief from his coat pocket (where it lay next to nothing more than an enamel snuff box), and loudly blew his nose.

"If mama were here to see what?" Lord James was mystified. His mother had died giving birth to a stillborn child when he was barely two years old and he had no recollection of her. The reference to St. George's (the fashionable church for *ton* weddings) had escaped him entirely, and he had given up trying to answer all the questions his sire peppered him with.

"Your nuptials, my boy! Your wedding!"

"My wedding?" exclaimed his son. "Whom am I marrying ? Do I know her?"

"Whatever can you mean? Your Miss Maxwell, of course! You just told me the two of you have discussed children. You are a sly one! How long have you known her? Now, when are we to meet her?"

"I don't think Miss Maxwell knows we are to be married," said James. "I only met her today and she didn't mention it."

His father looked at him in horror, collapsed abruptly into his chair and put his head in his hands.

James waited for him to look up and when he didn't, said, "I don't want to pull caps with you, father, but if you've nothing more to say to me on the subject of my wedding may I talk to you about the new crop rotation I'd like to try in the Top Fields at Maylands? I've mentioned it before, but you didn't seem interested."

"Oh, very well," said his father, looking up at last, "I see it's hopeless to try to make you think of anything but your plans for the estate. I suppose I'd better hear you out." He settled ungraciously back in his chair and looked up at his son without any apparent pleasure.

James sat in front of him at the desk, and taking his notebook and stubby pencil from his pocket, spoke with real enthusiasm, illustrating his words with careful drawings.

"We presently rotate the sowing in parcels of three, and we leave one-third fallow every year. This means we can only harvest two-thirds of the land. Of the two-thirds that is cultivated, one-third is sown with grain for human consumption, and one with hay for livestock feed. One-third produces nothing." He divided a notebook page into three sections, in one drew what were clearly ears of wheat, in another clumps of clover, and left the third empty.

"But if we moved to a rotation of *four*: wheat, turnips, barley, and clover hay," and here he turned over the page, divided it into four, in two sections again drew the wheat and the clover then in the other two drew first a plant similar to the wheat but with thinner ears, then a series of very recognizable turnips, "each replenishes the soil for the next." He drew a large black circular arrow. "We have no fallow, we can harvest two types of grain to sell every year *and* two types of livestock feed. The clover and turnips would allow us to breed all year, and with the increased supply of fodder, achieve much better cattle weights. I should like to try the system in the Top Fields. If it is successful, we can extend it to the other fields in a year or so."

His father looked at his notebook page and shrugged his shoulders. "Where you get all this from, I don't know," he said. "But I'll take your word for it. I've always left that type of thing to Fletcher, you'd best take it up with him. But I suppose I have no objection."

Though this was hardly an enthusiastic response, James was delighted. He stood and bowed with a wide grin on his face.

"Thank you father. I'll start on it right away! And I'll... er, think about the other thing. The heir."

"I wish you'd be as enthusiastic about planting your own seed," grumbled the Marquess as he left the study. "A grandson would make me much happier than a field of turnips any day."

But it was too late. James didn't hear him. He had already left.

Chapter Three

James's father much preferred London to the country, and was happy to stay in the capital most of the year. But his son loved the land. He went back to Maylands, the Farrell estate in Middlesex, full of plans for the future. He immediately set to work on his new rotation system for the Top Fields, ignoring the shaking head of the land agent Fletcher, who grumbled that what had been all right for his father and his father's father before him should be all right. He completely forgot that he had said he would think about the necessity of finding a wife to produce the necessary heir.

The only thing that invariably drew the Marquess to Maylands was the hunt. He prided himself on being a fearless rider to hounds and never missed an opportunity to show off himself and his latest mount. It was nearly the end of the hunting season, but he had recently been delighted when an old rival put his huge hunter up for sale at Tattersall's, complaining that the beast had an odd kick in its gait. The truth, the Marquess knew, was that the horse was simply too unreliable for his rider. He had this information from his head groom, who had it from a drinking companion, who had it from a lad who worked in the seller's stables.

"Never been trained proper," was the assessment. "Just as likely to refuse at a gate as go over with a mile to spare. 'Is lordship gone arse over tit off 'im twice and that's it. 'E's 'ad enough."

The Marquess proclaimed the horse hadn't been born who could have *him* off, and announced his desire to buy the miscreant at any price. James was himself an excellent rider and whip, but not reckless like his father. He mistrusted the new hunter and begged his father to give up the idea.

"If the horse has been allowed to persist in his ways this long, it will be very difficult to re-train him. You should not attempt it. There are plenty of others to choose from. Besides, you'll hardly get to ride him this year. The season's almost over."

"Nonsense, my boy," replied his sire. "You are too nice. The animal simply needs to know who is its master. Trust me, it will soon know."

At first, it seemed he was right. The hunter behaved impeccably. He sailed over hedge and stile, landing gracefully and without a stumble. But on the third time out, whether because the Marquess relaxed his guard or because the horse decided to have a little fun, it galloped at full speed towards a gate, urged on by his rider, then, at the last minute, refused. The Marquess was raised out of his saddle, his neck forward over that of the horse, and when the animal stopped, he did not. He was the one to sail over, landing not gracefully, but on his head. He broke his neck; death was instantaneous.

The Marquess' body was carried back to Farrell Court. James was in the study, buried in facts and figures about crop yields and animal weights and hardly looked up when the normally sedate old butler Prewitt burst in on him. At first, he had trouble paying attention to what the man was saying and when he did, had no idea what to say or do.

"I... er, I...," he began.

Prewitt had known James since he was born and felt sorry for him. He had always been a kind boy, never demanding and peremptory like his father. "Naturally, you will want to see your father's, er... body, sir," he suggested. "Then Mrs. Varilly will be at your disposal. She will see to the, er... laying out of his lordship." He was referring to the housekeeper, who, like him, had known James all his life. They had both been with the house long enough to remember the death of James's mother. "She will know who to call in from the village. And you will want to write a note to the Reverend Austin, though I dare say he has already heard the news. He will arrange for his late lordship to be placed in the church for twenty-four hours before the funeral and interment. He will talk to you about the vigil. There will be no lack of volunteers to sit by the coffin in the church overnight. Naturally, you may choose when you wish to be there yourself. They will toll the big bell, of course, one for every year of his lordship's life. That way the locals will know who has ...er, passed away, if they haven't heard already."

He paused for a moment, then continued. "It will be necessary to send a note to his lordship's brother and one to the newspapers, and one to his lordship's... er, *your* solicitor, for the reading of the Will." The old man looked at him sympathetically. " We are all very sorry, my lord, that such a thing should happen." Privately, the butler thought it was surprising the late Marquess hadn't broken his neck before. He had always been reckless on a horse.

James looked at him, surprised at being called *my lord*. Then he realized he was the Marquess. He squared his shoulders.

"Thank you, Prewitt." He gave his brief but charming smile. "I should like to see my father now. And then please send Mrs. Varilly to me."

For James, the days following the death of his father were a nightmare. He was not a person who dealt well with change and suddenly everything was upside down. The front door bell was constantly being pulled as people called in or sent notes of condolence. He was asked questions he did not know how to answer, from the type of wood he wished for his father's coffin, to whether the psalms should be sung at the funeral service. This was a controversial question that the rector did not feel he should act upon unilaterally, but James just spread his hands in a gesture of uncertainty. He was so distracted by it all, he couldn't have told you in the end whether the psalms were sung or spoken.

His uncle and cousin turned up at Maylands. It disturbed him to find them in odd corners of the fine old home, looking at everything in a proprietorial fashion. He couldn't understand it. Then one day, Eustace, a weak-mouthed individual dressed in the height of fashion with a starched collar so high he could hardly turn his head, and tight yellow pantaloons entirely out of place in the country, tittered that he supposed since James was five years his senior and still unmarried, he might one day be master of Maylands himself. James looked at him in some surprise. He had entirely forgotten his father's words.

But that was nothing to the shock he was to receive after the funeral. He had just endured the funeral breakfast with all and sundry tramping through the home that was usually his haven of tranquility. He couldn't wait for people to leave and was wondering how he could get rid of his uncle and cousin, when Prewitt found him hiding in his study. He was looking longingly at the papers of facts and figures he hadn't been able to get back to for a week, but the butler told him the family solicitor, Mr. Sanderson, was in the morning room and waiting for him.

"Ah, there you are, my lord," said the dusty-looking man, when James presented himself. The solicitor was thin as a herring and looked as though he put himself away on the shelf with his papers at night. "Now we are all here, I shall read the Will. I should say, his late lordship made certain important changes only a month or so ago." He nodded towards James's uncle and cousin, "I'm glad you are here, sirs, as the changes affect you."

He drew his pince-nez from his pocket, undid the ribbon holding the stiff vellum, unrolled it and cleared his throat. There was the normal preamble followed by the expected bequests, then:

"To my only son James Alfred Percy Farrell, I bequeath the rest of my estate, both entailed and unentailed, and the income derived from it, including Maylands, Farrell Court and the London residence, together with such bank accounts and investments as I may hold at the time of my death,"

and here the solicitor drew in his breath and expelled it, saying loudly,

"ON CONDITION that he marry within four months of my funeral. If he fail to do so, I bequeath the unentailed portion of Maylands, namely what is known as the Top Fields, to my brother Ronald Anthony Percy Farrell, together with a lifetime usufruct of Farrell Court. My son James will retain only Farrell House in London and my bank accounts and investments. The use of Farrell Court will return to him after the death of my brother."

There was total silence in the room until James said slowly, "I'm not sure I heard correctly. Please will you read the last part again?"

The solicitor did as he was asked, and this time when he finished Eustace gave one of his characteristic titters. "'Pon my soul, James," he said. "That puts you under the gun, what? Four months to find a woman, woo her and marry her, or you lose a good portion of the estate, and use of the Court. And while you're wearing a black armband, too. But perhaps you don't think it's worth it? You've never been in the petticoat line, after all."

His cousin stared at him with his impenetrable black gaze for a moment, then said, "I may never have, as you put it, been in the petticoat line, but if that's what I must do to retain total control of the Farrell estates, you may be assured I shall find a woman, woo her and marry her within the prescribed period. The rest of it—the bank accounts, the investments, the house in London—I am tied to only by my title. But the land is my life's blood. It is all I care about. I intend to make the whole of it the most productive in Middlesex, if not in the country. Now, if you will excuse me, I have business to attend to. Please ring Prewitt for anything you require." He stood, gave a brief bow and left the room.

"By God," said his uncle. "For a moment there, I thought it was his father speaking. Know what, Eustace, I think our James will surprise us yet."

Chapter Four

The new Marquess strode straight into the study and shut the door. He was furious. He had always known that the Top Fields were unentailed, but, as far as he was aware, they had always passed to the heir anyway. It had never occurred to him that they might be willed away. It was only by the greatest effort of will that he did not slam the door and throw across the room the ornate silver candelabrum that had stood on the desk for years. But he controlled himself.

When he was a boy he had been subject to fits of rage, chiefly when he was told he wasn't old enough to do whatever it was he wanted to do, but also because other people so often seemed not to understand him, nor he them. He frequently threw things across the room, and often they were things he most valued. Then he would cry hot tears of anger mixed with sorrow, sobbing that they didn't understand; he didn't want to be a boy, he didn't want to be told he could not do something because he was too young. He wasn't too young, he wasn't.

His nanny, a woman with a good deal of experience, understood and dearly loved him. She would hold him tight and soothe him, but not say anything. Then, when he was calm enough to listen, she would try to explain. "Now listen, James," she told him, "when you throw things and rage as you do, you only succeed in proving to people that you *are* just a boy. Grown men know how to control themselves. When you can control yourself, you'll know you are a man, and other people will know too."

It was not a lesson he learned quickly or easily. He had moved on from his nanny to a tutor before he knew what she had said was right. Once he was out of the nursery, he received more than one whipping both from his tutor and his father for having broken something valuable in one of his rages. He was indifferent to the whippings themselves, but after a while he realized it was only because people considered him nothing but a boy that he was punished in such a demeaning way. No one would dare to do it if he were a man.

He began to control himself; he dug his nails into his palms, he gritted his teeth, he forced himself to control his breathing. Those around him, particularly his father, congratulated themselves on having taught him better. But he knew it was all his nanny's doing; she had told him what he needed to do. And finally, he did.

His nanny had been retired to a cottage on the estate for many years now, but James still went to see her regularly. He went there now. She had not been at the funeral; it was rare for women to attend funerals, and she was anyway disabled by rheumatism.

He knocked on her door calling out, as he always did, "It's only me, Nanny, don't get up!"

He went into her small parlor, cluttered with objects she had been given over the years, mostly by him. Amongst them were a number of things he had made when he was a boy: little plaster of Paris figures, carefully painted, a curiously-shaped twig he had found and carved into the head of a horse, a tiny but complete skull of a vole he had found on one of their walks. These humble objects were her pride and joy, even more than the Norwich silk shawl, the brass fender with the leather top she could put her feet up on in front of the fire and the other more costly things he bought her when he grew up.

He caught her trying to stand up as he came in "My lord," she said, "and on the very day of the funeral! You should not have left your visitors!"

"Don't get up, Nanny, I told you. And I'm not *my lord*. I'm your James, the same as I always was. And damn the visitors." Then he fell to his knees beside her. "Nanny, tell me what to do!"

He explained the provisions of his father's Will, his anger rising again as he did so.

"I swear I'll contest it!" he said. "Anyone can see he must have been mad when he wrote it! Four months to get married, or I lose the very land I've been working on all these months! No man can be expected to find a good wife in that time, especially as I have to be in mourning and can't go about to all the parties and so on. What did he think I could do?"

"Now, now," she said calmly. "What can't be mended can't be helped. 'Tis a peculiar thing to have put in his Will, but seemingly your father thought he'd never bring you to marriage any other way. He knew you love the land and you'd do anything to keep it. And I daresay he thought you'd be more likely to find a suitable wife at quiet evenings than loud, public affairs."

"He just wanted to bully me as much after his death as he did before. But I'll show him! I'll marry the first woman I see. It will probably be the milkmaid!"

Nanny laughed. "Nonsense," she said, fondly. "Parties or no parties, once the mamas realize you're in town and looking for a wife, they'll be contriving ways of throwing their daughters at your feet before you can say knife, as good-looking and as rich as you are! And a Marquess besides. Why! You'll have your choice. Just decide whether you want her tall or short, dark or fair! Besides pretty, of course."

"I don't want her at all!" cried James. "All they talk about is dances and dresses!"

Nanny laughed again. "You just haven't met the right one. You must get in touch with all your old school chums and tell them you're in need of cheering up. Most of them are married—I see the announcements in the Court Circular all the time. Their wives probably know a host of pretty girls. And if they're still single, their mamas will. They'll know you can't go dancing or anything like that while you're wearing a black armband."

He looked very doubtful, remembering more than one boring evening sat next to someone's niece or sister at a dinner party, but Nanny patted his hand. "It will all come right, you'll see. And she'll be a lucky girl. You will make a fine husband. Nanny knows."

He spent another half hour with her, talking about her annual trip to her sister's in Worthing, where she spent a month by the sea. "And don't the neighbors still gawk when they see me coming and going in a Farrell coach!" she said with satisfaction. "You are so good to me, my lord."

"No better than you deserve, Nanny," he responded with his charming smile. "Without you, I'd still be throwing candlesticks at the walls."

When he left he felt much better. He always did.

A few days later he left for London, having done as Nanny advised. He had written to as many friends as he thought might be able to help him. He simply said that he'd been blue-devilled in the country since his father's death, and needed cheering up. They would understand.

They did. Once he was back in the city, invitations began to arrive thick and fast. He was obliged to refuse a few: a dance party at Almack's was out of the question, a moonlit ridotto likewise. But he sat through any number of dinner parties, soirées described as quiet evening with friends, of which the chief function seemed to be to show off the unwed maidens, and many dull concerts. For these, the programs seemed to have been designed specially for someone in mourning and if he had actually listened to any of it would have been more depressed than ever. As it was, he spent the time thinking about the promising results beginning to show at Maylands and dreading having to give it up. He couldn't have named a single composer he had heard.

One enterprising matron proposed an improving lecture followed by a light supper. This was the one event that actually interested James. It dealt with the popular science of phrenology. The lecturer asserted that the brain was made up of different organs which were developed to a greater or lesser degree depending on the character of the individual. Calling for a volunteer, he thoroughly examined the man's head with his fingertips, and declared a cranial bump over his left ear showed him to be of a prudent disposition. Since this was rather more flattering than otherwise, the individual accepted it readily enough.

"He probably will be prudent the rest of his life," commented James to no one in particular. "So we'll never know which came first, the bump or the characteristic."

But Deborah Turnbull, daughter of his hostess who had, naturally enough, been placed next to him, heard what he said.

"Oh, don't you believe in it, then?" she said, turning wide eyes upon him.

He fixed her with his stare. "I think I'd need a good deal more evidence. It doesn't sound like science to me."

She was abashed by his steady gaze, but her mama had told her to engage him if she could. So she said, "I'm not sure I understand you, but if you say so, I'm sure you are right."

"Why?" James was genuinely puzzled.

How was she to explain that her mama had impressed on her she must agree with what a gentleman said, especially if she didn't quite understand it. "Well, I... er, I know nothing of the matter. I'm sure you are better informed than I."

"But I knew nothing of it either until coming here this evening. We have both had the same opportunity to absorb the information. I know no more or less than you."

"But gentlemen are naturally more able to... to make judgements."

"Why?" James asked again. His gaze didn't waver; he was not being argumentative. He found this very interesting.

The poor girl was almost in a panic. This was not how gentlemen were supposed to behave. They were supposed to accept their own superiority. After all, they went to school and university. Girls did not.

"I... I don't know," she said finally. "At least," she decided to ignore mama's advice and say what she felt. "You have the advantage of going to Eton or Harrow or somewhere, and probably the university. You have learned to have judgement, have you not?"

Thinking back on his education, James rather wondered what exactly it was he had learned. He had certainly translated a good deal of Greek and Latin. Had that made him able to form good judgements?

"That is a very good question," he said, giving her his rare charming smile. "I don't know the answer to it. But we were earlier talking about evidence. Here is some, at least. Most of the men in parliament have been educated as you describe, but they often make very stupid decisions. So one may say with some degree of certainty that education at Eton and Oxford, or Harrow and Cambridge, if you like, does not guarantee any degree of good judgement."

The young lady gave a timid smile. She wasn't sure whether one should talk in such a way about the men in government. They were surely very superior gentlemen indeed. She knew her papa would not like to hear her agreeing with Lord Farrell on this point. But it made her feel pleasantly *fast* to do so.

Later on, when her bosom bow Annie Frimpton asked her what she and the Marquess had been talking about after the lecture, she said airily, "Oh, politics, you know!"

"Stuff!" said Annie. "You don't know any more about politics than I do. I believe he was making love to you, you sly thing!"

"No he wasn't!" said Deborah. "He spent most of the time staring at me and asking why I said what I did! He is so odd!"

But then she thought, perhaps that *was* his idea of making love. He *did* have a charming smile, but she couldn't imagine him making love to her in the way she had heard young men did. He wouldn't bring her a posy of violets or a beautifully lettered verse of poetry, would he? And he was not at all comfortable to be with. Could one sigh on his bosom and lift one's lips for a kiss? He would probably ask *why?* and just stare.

Later, when her papa asked her the same question as Annie, she gave the same answer.

"*Politics?*" he was incredulous. "What's the feller want to talk about politics for?"

"And I fear he may be, well, a *radical*, Papa. He said the men in government were stupid."

"Good lord! I don't say he may not be right, in some cases, but that he should talk to you about it..." Mr. Turnbull, who had political aspiration himself, shook his head. Good thing the girl didn't seem much *épris* with the man. It wouldn't do to have a radical in the family, no matter how much money he might have.

"I shouldn't encourage him, my dear," he said to his daughter. "I don't think I could give my consent there."

"No, Papa, I won't. Anyway, he is so very odd! He stares so at one."

The new Marquess left the soirée quite pleased that he'd actually had a conversation with a young woman, though for the moment he couldn't remember her name. He thought it began with a D. Diana, was it?

Chapter Five

When James had continued on his way towards the bookshelves in The Temple Of The Muses, Miss Maxwell looked for a while at his departing back then shook her head and returned to her task of looking for images of the Tahitian Islands. Although both Spanish and British explorers had discovered Tahiti years before him, it was the Frenchman Louis-Antoine de Bougainville's account of his landing there in 1767 that caused a sensation in Europe. She had found a copy of his book, *A Voyage Around The World,* in the original French. She couldn't find it in English, though she knew a translation had been published. She thanked God for her old governess's insistence that she learn French, for she could read it well enough. But she drew in her breath sharply at the price of fifteen shillings, and knew she could never buy it. She had been hoping to find something cheaper in one of the drawers, a pamphlet perhaps, but no luck.

Surreptitiously, she scanned the book for images that she could copy. There were drawings of the pretty flowering vine *bougainvillea* named for the French explorer, and of the handsome island people wearing a sort of skirt of brightly colored cloth. She spent as much time copying as she dared, then replaced the book, promising herself to return in a day or two.

On subsequent trips to the bookstore she avidly read de Bougainville's account of how the native people welcomed the explorers. They brought them baskets of fruit, along with pigs, hens and ells of the bright cloth they wore. She smiled to herself imagining the illustrations she could devise showing pigs and hens on the ships.

The explorer wrote that when the travelers ventured into the interior of the island they thought themselves in a veritable garden of Eden. Orchards full of fruit and slim gum trees grew wild, apparently needing no cultivation to make them fruitful. In her imagination, she drew pictures of people in those bright skirts picnicking beneath them, the green grass below and the blue sky above. What a contrast to the grey colors of London!

When the island people saw the strangers gathering edible green plants to ward off scurvy, the plague of seafaring men, they brought them basketfuls of the same, along with quantities of shellfish. The sailors paid them with nails and metal tools. What an interesting concept for children to learn, she thought. To be paid with something one could use, rather than with money, which was worth nothing in itself and would have been useless to the islanders.

She was just thinking she had enough material for her little book, when a clerk, who had been eying her suspiciously for some days, bustled up.

"I've noticed you reading that book for some days, Miss," he said pompously. "If you intend to read more, may I suggest you buy it? Otherwise, kindly replace it on the shelves. There's others may like to purchase it, if you do not."

"Thank you," said Ellie, with a bright smile. "I had to study it closely. It's in French, you see." She waved the book under his nose. "But once I'd worked out what it was all about, I saw it was not what I wanted at all. But I'm grateful to you, anyway. You're very kind."

Since being kind was the last thing the clerk had intended, he did not know how to answer. He smiled wanly and took the book she was handing to him.

"Yes, Miss... er...," he said, ultimately unable to answer her lovely smile of thanks with anything more churlish.

"Maxwell, Elisabeth Maxwell," she replied, adding with more wishful thinking than strict accuracy, "author of children's books." And taking her gloves from her reticule, she walked out of the shop, pulling them on as she went.

Chapter Six

Ellie made her way home, deep in thought. None of those thoughts centered on James Farrell. She was wondering about her future. She had been born into a family of minor aristocracy; her father had been a Baron with a small, not very profitable estate in Berkshire. The more valuable land had been sold off at intervals by her grandfather and his father before him, neither man being able to say no to a wager or, it appeared, pick a winning horse. Her father had been an amiable, kind man who had none of the vices of his forebears, but was not very businesslike either. They had managed to live well enough on what the estate brought in, though as a family they spent little time there, not having sufficient income to make the necessary repairs. Instead he leased a townhouse on the edge of fashionable Mayfair in London. He loved his wife and daughter and never for a moment had wished she'd been a son to carry on the title.

Then, when she was fourteen years old, her father had developed some mysterious illness of the blood and had dwindled away to nothing before their eyes. After his death, Elisabeth had been brought to the realization that the comfortable, though by no means luxurious, way of life she had taken for granted was now beyond their means. And the lack of an heir was now keenly felt. The Baron's brother inherited the title and the estate, and the modest income that went with it. He left the army and took his pension. Together with the revenue from the estate, this was enough to make the repairs needed to the family home, but not enough to support the London household as well. He allowed his brother's relict to keep the townhome, on which the lease was due to expire anyway in six years, but gave her nothing to live on. The Dowager Baroness had a little money of her own which enabled them to live with a modicum of comfort. But she did not have the means either to introduce her daughter into society or buy the lease on a new home. Ellie's mother had been a beauty and was still a pretty woman, but she had neither the upbringing nor the natural inclination to manage money, or consider how to earn more.

It was this situation that had caused Ellie to try to find a way to make a living. She had, of course, thought of marriage. A well-to-do husband would solve all their problems. The trouble was, never having had her coming-out and consequently being unknown in London society, Ellie had no chance of meeting the sort of man she felt would suit her. She had been raised a gentlewoman. The clerks and managers she met while dealing with her mother's affairs might have been interested in her, but she was not interested in them.

She had been reared with a governess and decided it would be a good occupation for herself, as she was quite bookish. But when she mentioned it to her mother, the Dowager wept bitterly at the very suggestion. She had lost her beloved husband, she said, and could not bear to lose her daughter as well. Then the idea of writing children's books had slowly taken root. Ellie felt she had as good a chance of succeeding with that as with anything.

The years remaining on the lease were almost up, and the loss of their home was looming imminently when fate took a hand. The owners of the property, anxious to sell a new lease as soon as the old one was up, brought Mr. Cornelius Brownlow, a wealthy widower, to look over the premises. He was a well-to-do wine merchant who had family on the Kentish coast. By taking advantage of smuggled liquors and wines, he had been able to keep his cellars more cheaply stocked than those of his competitors during Bonaparte's rampages through Europe, and had amassed a fortune. He was looking for a house in a fashionable district, and while the Maxwell address was not one of the absolute best, it satisfied Mr. Brownlow's desire for value for money.

What satisfied him even more was the pretty widow. The Dowager's quiet and ladylike demeanor convinced him that here was the wife he needed to replace his dear dead Emily, and, moreover, help him into a society he felt he now deserved. He called Ellie's mother *dear lady* and treated her as if she were a piece of bone china, tenderly helping her into his carriage when their relationship moved to the level of going for a drive together. The widow recognized that, while her suitor was not quite out of the top drawer, here was a broad chest to lean upon. This led her to accept his offer of marriage.

She and Mr. Brownlow were married with considerable pomp at London's Guildhall, and settled back into the London townhouse, on which a very advantageous lease had been signed. Mr. Brownlow augmented the household staff, which had been reduced to a butler, a cook, a single maid and his wife's dresser. They now had a kitchen maid and a footman. He encouraged his wife to hold dinner parties. The new Mrs. Brownlow asked the same people she had been wont to invite when her husband was alive. If a few of the invitees refused on the ostensible basis of prior engagements, and the ones who did come seemed more interested in the good prices they could obtain to replenish their wine cellars than in returning the invitation, Mr. Brownlow was satisfied.

What he was not satisfied with was Elisabeth. He found her managing and pert, and was conscious that every time she looked at him she saw right through him to his humble origins on a farm in Kent. Accustomed to her gentlemanly father, it was true that Ellie found Mr. Brownlow a poor replacement. He was kind to her mother, who accepted without demur his desire to be involved in every decision made in the household, from the purchase of a new hat for his wife, to the grade of tallow candles used in the kitchen. With Ellie it was otherwise.

"Elisabeth, my dear," he would say, in a tone that told her a veiled reprimand was coming, "I wish you would use that new reticule I gave you rather than the old thing you persist in carrying. 'Pon my soul, you look no better than the coalsmith's daughter with that!"

"But sir," she had replied more than once, "this reticule is large enough for my notebook and pencils. The one you gave me is exceedingly pretty and I thank you again for it, but it will hold nothing more than a handkerchief."

"A young lady should need nothing more than a handkerchief," he retorted, unconsciously echoing the Marquess. "It beats me why you need a notebook and pencils. The next thing is," again echoing the Marquess, with whom he would have been delighted to know he had a good deal in common, "they'll be saying you're a bluestocking!" He gave a forced bellow of laughter.

"They, whoever *they* are, may say what they like," replied Ellie, tartly. "I need to make notes for my books, and there's an end to it."

When her mother began to remonstrate gently with her, saying she should try not to displease her stepfather, Ellie knew something would have to be done. If only she could publish her book and earn enough money to move out!

Over the next two months she completed her Tahiti book. She wrote it from the point of view of Pierre, a twelve-year old cabin boy who left St. Malo in 1766 on board de Bougainville's frigate *Boudeuse*. She imagined Pierre writing a diary to record his experiences. He recounted his adventures in a way that was comprehensible, Ellie hoped, to a child of about seven, expressing fear, joy and amazement at the various things he saw. To accompany the text Ellie painted watercolors, using the illustrations she adapted from de Bougainville's own diary, or simply her imagination. She was proud of the finished product: a beautifully colored little book of about twenty pages.

Unfortunately, it appeared that proud as she may be of her work, no one else was remotely interested. She took it in turn to all the publishers in London—from the largest to the smallest—and was met everywhere with shaken heads.

"The market is awash in children's stories, and because of the illustrations, they're expensive to produce," explained Mr. Woolstone, of Woolstone & Browne, one of the smaller houses. "Now, if you were to pay the production costs, we could print a few and see how it goes."

"Oh dear," said Elisabeth. "That's not how I imagined it at all! I was hoping you would pay me!"

"That simply isn't possible, Miss... er, Maxwell. We cannot tie up capital like that. I'm sorry."

Richard Forsythe, a slim, handsome though rather foppish young man, employed as typesetter in the establishment, had overheard the conversation. He was of a very romantic disposition. Indeed, Miss Turnbull, who had found James so unlike the suitors she had read about, would have thought Mr. Forsythe a perfect example. He wrote sweet verses in his spare moments and would certainly thrust well-chosen posies into the hands of his beloved. He was touched by Ellie's predicament. He saw her outmoded bonnet and pelisse as signs of an impoverished lady artist and wished fate had made him a man of means so he could rescue her. *Elisabeth Maxwell,* he would remember the name.

Not knowing that at least one personable young man was wishing he could help her, Ellie went home, as despondent as someone with her natural optimism could be. Her mood wasn't lightened by the knowledge that her mother and stepfather were entertaining that evening and she would be called on to stop the conversation from flagging.

Her stepfather's idea of conversation was to make declarations in a loud voice, usually followed by a boom of laughter. The botched attempts to rescue passengers from the French ship *Medusa* that had run aground near the coast of West Africa was on the front pages of all the papers. Tonight he pronounced, "Well, the French! What do you expect? Couldn't rescue a cat from a tree, what?" Her mother made a gentle remark about the poor people who drowned, and a gloom seemed about to fall over the company.

Ellie racked her brains and finally asked the table at large, "What is the latest *on dit* about Prince Leopold and Princess Charlotte? How do they go on?"

"Dear Princess Charlotte!" said one matron. "They seem very happy together. I understand she is already in an interesting condition. Let us hope it will come to a happy conclusion!"

"Indeed," chimed in another. "It was shameful the way the Regent bullied her into a betrothal before she found Saxe-Coburg!"

"Yes! Making her accept the Prince of Orange was the height of folly," came a response. "After all, she is heir to the British throne! She has always said she won't leave England, and the prince wanted her to live in Holland! Anyone could see that wouldn't work!"

"Good thing she broke the engagement," said someone. "Though I don't believe the story about her being in love with the

Duke of Gloucester. Do you remember the newspaper headline: *Will it be The Orange Or The Cheese*? Too funny!"

"Not very funny for her!" chided the first matron, obviously a Charlotte sympathizer. "Her father had her all but locked up at Windsor!"

"That's what they said, but it seems she saw as many men as she wanted. Her mother even encouraged it. Just to get back at the Regent, of course."

There was a sharp intake of breath around the table at this. Suggesting that the princess wasn't, well, as good as she should be, really, some people went too far. But it could go further, apparently.

"Well, there was that story she liked to go around the palace with her... let's just say *unmentionables,* showing around her ankles."

There was scandalized laughter, but the sympathizer was loud in Charlotte's defense. "That was when she was only a girl! She is a perfectly proper, lovely young woman now. God bless her! And when she met Leopold of Saxe-Coburg, it was love at first sight. We should all wish them very happy!"

"They should be happy, by God!" This was Ellie's stepfather. "Parliament gave Saxe-Coburg fifty thousand a year plus Claremont House!"

"Pretty good for him to endow her with all his worldly goods!" added one of the other gentlemen. "What worldly goods? He hasn't a groat we haven't given him!"

And so the chatter went on. Ellie was able to sit back and simply smile from one speaker to the other. The past, present and future of the newly married royal couple was thoroughly discussed until it was time for the ladies to leave the gentlemen to their port. Even then, amongst the women it continued, with speculation as to whether the princess would carry her pregnancy to term. She had been taken ill at the opera the other day, and one had to wonder.

Chapter Seven

"I think, my dear," said Mrs. Brownlow quietly to her husband one morning not long after the dinner party, "if you don't object, we need to think about poor Ellie's future. She is a dear girl, and so lively. I know she would like to support herself with her writing, but really, every girl needs a husband."

She smiled up at her big husband as she said this. Heaven knows, he wasn't a gentleman like her poor dead Robert, but he was strong and reliable and could be counted on to provide for her.

"Of course she needs a husband," he responded, "But how is she going to get one, acting like a bluestocking as she does? Carrying notebooks and pencils in that great sack of hers?"

"Well, of course, she is very clever and we couldn't afford a coming out, so...," then, as her husband went to interrupt her, "no, no, I'm not proposing that now. The cost of a court dress alone is prohibitive. But I do think she could be introduced in a quiet way if she had a couple of new gowns. My old friend Martha Penhale is Ellie's godmother. I think she would undertake it. She's the dowager widow of Lord Penhale and everyone knows her."

Mr. Brownlow's eyes lit up as he considered the social advantage of having a stepdaughter being brought out by a Lady, even if she was the dowager. "Well," he harrumphed, "it could be done, I suppose."

"There would be some cost, of course. As I said, she will need new gowns and... and dance lessons. The waltz, you know, is all the rage these days, and the quadrilles have far more set pieces than the old cotillions we learned in my day. She couldn't be introduced into society not knowing those. It would be too shaming to have to sit by the wall while the other girls dance!"

"I've no objections to a few gowns, within reason, and I trust you for that. As for dance lessons, why, I wouldn't object to them myself. If we are to go to balls and the like, it would be as well we know the new steps ourselves."

Mrs. Brownlow winced inwardly at the idea of her lumbering husband making a cake of himself on the dance floor. But she loved her daughter and thought even that would be not too big a price to pay to see her settled. So she went to see her friend Martha Penhale and the two ladies discussed together what was best to be done.

"We cannot think of Almack's," said that lady. "Mr. Brownlow's er, background, would make that impossible."

They both knew the lady patrons of that popular but tonnish establishment would never allow across its hallowed portals a person from the merchant class.

"But," she continued, I think I can persuade Monty to have a ball at Penhale House. That wife of his will be glad to host it if he loosens his purse strings for once. I have a, well, let's say, an important birthday this year and I can use that as an excuse to introduce my god-daughter. It won't be a massive affair, but enough for dear Ellie to be presented to the right people. We'll have her betrothed by the end of the year! Mark my words!"

"Oh, Martha!' replied her friend with relief, "how grateful I am to you! When poor Robert died I was at my wits' end, as you know. Cornelius was like a savior to me, although, well…," she faltered.

Her friend patted her hand. "I know, my dear, I know. It isn't easy. We widows have to do what we must. Talking of that, did you hear that Suzie Smithers was left..."

And they enjoyed a cozy gossip about mutual acquaintances, some better, some worse off, but many forced to navigate the uneasy shoals of widowhood. Gentlemen seemed to die so much earlier than their wives. Why, they wondered? It was a mystery.

There followed for Elisabeth a period she told herself she shouldn't enjoy so much, for she liked to think herself above such things, but in fact she did. She went to her mama's long-time dressmaker, a woman who called herself Hélène but in fact hailed from Surrey. She was a woman of excellent but thrifty taste who had made a career of creating gowns for women whose husbands could not, or would not, pay a great deal to clothe their wives. Most of her clients were older women. It was a treat for her to dress Ellie, who, while she was no beauty, was slim and rather above average height, and consequently added distinction to the simplest gown. Her brown hair and pale blue eyes were unremarkable, but her real beauty, apart from the liveliness of her expression, was a lovely creamy complexion that owed nothing to Denmark Lotion or nightly bathings with rose water.

The *modiste* immediately recognized that dresses in light shades would best become her. White was out of the question, although ivory, if exactly the right color and not too yellow, was a possibility. The ladies spent a pleasurable afternoon looking through ells of silk and muslin, then Madame's books of patterns. They decided on a ballgown featuring a simple pale pink silk sheath with cap sleeves, scoop necked and decorated beneath the bosom with a band of white lace, which, fortunately, Madame had left over from another order. It had a matching filmy overdress with a train that could be caught up on the wrist for dancing.

"One may run up another under gown in ivory and use the same overdress. Then, if one matches the gloves to the dress, the ensembles will look quite different, you'll see."

For an evening dress, they chose a pale blue silk, exactly the color of Ellie's eyes. Again, it was quite simple, enhanced with just a darker blue band under the bosom and with narrow sleeves to just above the elbow. The plainer the better, declared Madame. Anything more, and people would remember one wore it last time.

She persuaded them to purchase two silk shawls, one embroidered and one plain. Again, if worn alternately with the simple evening dress, they would create quite a different look. After all, she said, apart from balls, one spent evenings mostly sitting down, and it was the top half that mattered. The shawls were not of the first quality Norwich silk, though one had to look hard to know the difference. Mrs. Brownlow felt this would be a good selling point for her husband.

Finally, they chose two day dresses, one in pale pink sprigged muslin and the other in a finely striped blue. The plain shawl would work with both. Not the embroidered one; that would be too much for daywear.

"I think," said her mother after this orgy, "tomorrow we will go to Pantheon Bazaar. We will buy gloves and a little thing or two to put in your hair. Perhaps also some buckles for your slippers. Madame is quite right, one needs very little to alter one's appearance. I've been doing it for years."

Ellie had never paid a great deal of attention to her appearance, but she now realized her mother was always well-dressed, even when they had very little money. *Hmm*, she suddenly thought, *there is more to being clever than reading books.*

The dance lessons, which she dreaded, turned out to be a success for the whole family. Luckily, the leased house had been built in the previous century, when the ladies' skirts were so wide that dwellings had to be built to accommodate them. This meant the reception rooms were larger than was currently the fashion. On the first floor there was a big, nearly empty room now almost never used, generally called the music room for the simple reason a pianoforte stood there. Ellie had had not very successful lessons on it when she was younger. They were something she had gratefully given up as soon as she could. The instrument was covered in a dust cloth and the room smelled musty.

Mr. Brownlow, having decided on something, characteristically threw himself into it. He liked the idea of dance lessons, so in a whirl, he had the fire lit, the carpet taken up, the room dusted, the chandeliers lowered, cleaned and filled with new wax candles (second grade) and the pianoforte dusted and tuned. He interviewed dance masters and their accompanists. He didn't want anyone too young or fashionable and likely to snigger at his capers, so settled in the end on a very thin, unprepossessing individual with exaggerated mannerisms and the unlikely name of Roland de Courcy. He arrived with a woman, as stout as he was lean, with round cheeks and a full bosom, who he introduced as both his wife and his accompanist.

"My wife was set for a career as a concert pianist, but her, er, appearance worked against her," he explained. "One expects a pianist to be thin and artistic-looking. My dear Elsie looks too jolly. But she is a magnificent performer."

This proved to be true for them both. Mrs. de Courcy ran her fingers expertly over the keys and launched into a flowing waltz that threw her husband into a graceful twirl around the room, holding an imaginary partner. His feet seemed to fly, his chin was high and his thin back arched like a swan. He was glorious to behold. His audience was rapt.

He was a very patient teacher, which was a good thing, as Mr. Brownlow was anything but an apt pupil. His wife bore her crushed toes with fortitude and wished he could get over the habit he developed of keeping time with the music by muttering *one, two, three-four, one, two, three-four* in her ear all the time he was waltzing, and by repeating *toe to your in, toe to your out, in two three, out two three, pas de basque, pas de basque, circle left, circle right,* or whatever set quadrille piece they were performing.

Elisabeth was generally partnered by Mr. de Courcy and found it very pleasurable indeed. He was an excellent dancer; he seemed to barely touch her or lead her in any direction, but she followed him without missing a step and without looking at her feet. It was otherwise when she relinquished the teacher to her poor mother and partnered her stepfather. He pushed and pulled as if she were a horse he was trying to lead into a stall, and if she looked at her feet it was because she was trying to keep them out of his way.

Nevertheless, they were all ready for Lady Penhale's ball when it came. They were introduced into the room by the Penhales' very solemn butler as *Mr. and Mrs. Brownlow and the Honorable Elisabeth Maxwell.*

Mr. Brownlow was indignant on his wife's behalf, "Why did he not call you Baroness?" he whispered.

"Because when I married you I lost the title. But it was worth it, my dear!" she whispered back, raising her eyes to his.

His cup was full. He was being presented to a ballroom full of lords and ladies with a daughter who was an honorable and a wife who used to be a dowager baroness but gladly gave up the title for him.

Chapter Eight

Ellie enjoyed the ball very much and had the pleasure of not sitting out a single dance. The dance master was assiduous in making sure unpartnered maidens were paired up as much as possible, but in Ellie's case his attentions were unnecessary. She looked pretty in her pink ballgown and her obvious enjoyment showed on her face. She danced gracefully and chatted in a friendly way to all the men who partnered her, so they never had the daunting task of drawing out a tongue-tied debutante. This in itself was enough to make her sought out. By the end of the evening, she was held to be a jolly good sort and the young men made sure their mothers invited her to whatever events they were planning.

The mantelpiece in the drawing room was soon loaded with cards of all shapes and sizes from visiting cards left by would-be suitors to invitations to dinners, concerts, informal dances and *just a quiet evening with friends* to the more daring picnic by the river and a masquerade at Vauxhall Gardens.

Her mother frowned at the last, but she need not have worried. After a month or so of all this, Ellie was becoming tired of the meaninglessness of it all. She recognized that her job, to be blunt about it, was to find a husband. But it was hopeless. Everything went fine at first, when she was just exchanging brief remarks during dances or at the intermission of concerts or the opera, but when the men who would have liked to court her sat by her side for longer conversations, she found them dull and predictable. Not one of them read the newspapers, it seemed. Not one had an original thought. They repeated what they'd heard in their clubs without enquiry as to whether it was accurate or not.

"It seems Byron and Shelley are in Italy and are writing a novel about a monster," one had said the week before. "Still, it must be better than all that love poetry you girls are wild about."

"I think you are mistaken," Ellie had replied. "I believe it's Shelley's wife Mary who has read from a piece she is working on about a monstrous creature called *Frankenstein*."

"Nonsense!" he had responded. "How could a woman write about such a thing? The female sensibility would not allow it."

"Why ever not?" she was outraged. "Women have to deal with horrors every bit as much as men, perhaps more. We are stronger than you think."

"Women deal with horrors?" he scoffed. "The ones I know live on silken cushions. It's we men who face the real difficulties of life."

Dealing with husbands like you would be horror enough, she thought but did not say. Instead, she smiled politely. Needless to say, that was the last she saw of him.

More trouble arose when she made the mistake of telling another about her writing aspirations. He had first described at length the latest carriage race he had taken part in. He told her in detail about the marvelous way he had feathered the corners on the prescribed course and caught his whip in his hand so as not to have the thong flying behind and touching the horses on their hind quarters.

"Takes some doing, I can tell you," he said "the thong is nearly four yards long!"

At last, he must have remembered some precept about not talking about himself all the time and said, "Do you ride or drive?"

"No," she smiled, "I'm afraid not. I am not very sportive. I'm fond of reading and writing. Especially writing. I've written a book for children, as a matter of fact, about de Bougainville's voyage to Tahiti."

"About whose voyage to where?" he seemed incredulous.

"Louis de Bougainville. He travelled around the world in the middle of the last century."

"A French cove, was he?"

"Yes, but his book is available in English. It's very interesting."

"Take your word for it. Not too keen on the Frogs. I say, you ain't a bluestocking, I hope? You don't look like one."

"Thank you!" she laughed. That evening she was wearing her blue evening dress with the embroidered silk shawl. This featured white roses, so into her hair she had twisted a length of small paper roses purchased at the Pantheon Bazaar. Her cavalier was right: she looked too pretty to be a bluestocking. "But if that means a woman who is bookish, I'm afraid I must be."

"Pity. I don't like to see a woman with her nose in a book, unless it's one of those novels you're all wild about.'

She laughed again. "Last week I was told we're all wild about love poetry, and now it's novels. 'Pon my word, you gentlemen have a poor view of us!"

Her interlocutor didn't know quite how to answer this and soon found an excuse to leave her. She thought nothing of it, but it turned out she had said the wrong thing to the wrong person. He had been a popular young man, quite one of the tulips of the *ton*, and when he put out the word that Miss Maxwell, jolly though she was, was a self-proclaimed bluestocking, the invitations began to drop off.

Mr. Brownlow heard about it and was furious. "God knows I dropped enough blunt to get her a husband, and then she goes around telling people she's writing a book about some French feller. Everyone's calling her a bluestocking! It's beyond enough!"

His wife tried to calm him, but his bad temper cast a pall over the household. Once again, Ellie was left wondering what on earth she was going to do.

Chapter Nine

James Farrell, Marquess of Hastings, had been in London over three months in search of a wife. His quest had been singularly unsuccessful. He had met a number of young women whom he had quite liked, but none of them had liked him. One or two had even seemed afraid of him. This had puzzled him, and he tried to explain to one maiden that he hadn't thrown anything in over fifteen years, but this did not appear to reassure her. He didn't realize it, but it was his black gaze she found unnerving, as did the others.

On the other hand, he was afraid of the women who appeared to be interested in him. They all seemed the same: very modern and sure of themselves. One bold-eyed damsel with progressive ideas told him straight out, "I know everyone says you stare and are very odd, but I don't care. You're good-looking and you're rich. That's enough for me. We'd have a marriage of convenience, in any case. I have no intention of being a slave to a man. We need not even live in the same house."

"A marriage of convenience?" It was not a term he was familiar with. "Convenient for whom?"

"For both of us. I don't pretend to love you, but there may be others I do love. Such a marriage would give us both the freedom to indulge those other... passions. I don't imagine you love me, do you?"

"Love you?" James gave it serious consideration, as he did with all questions he was asked. Then he turned his gaze upon her. "No, I don't."

"Perfect. Shall we set the date?"

"Date? What date?"

"The date of our wedding. I have to say, I would prefer it sooner rather than later. I long to have my own establishment. You won't mind if I make some changes to Farrell House, will you? Mama says it's dreadfully old-fashioned."

James was still working on the first part of this answer. Feeling cornered, he blurted out, "But I don't want to marry you! I don't even like you!"

"I don't like you much either," she replied calmly, "but, as I said, it will be of no consequence. We shall hardly ever see each other."

James suddenly had a clear memory of his father talking about heirs. "But what about children?"

"Oh, I expect I'll produce some. It's inevitable. No one will know if they're not yours."

He thought about that. Then, with complete clarity, he knew he would know and he would care. If he had children he wanted them to be his. "No," he said.

"There you are, then. You won't mind. As I said, it's perfect."

"No, yes, I *do* mind. I want my children to be my children. I shall want…," he searched for the word, "… a family."

The young woman looked at him in disgust. "How disappointingly banal your ideas are, after all," she spat, and stalked away.

He looked after her in some surprise, then shrugged his shoulders. What a strange young woman! Why should she have thought he would want to marry her? She didn't like him and he certainly didn't like her. And as for having other men's children, he didn't like children much to begin with, and he certainly wouldn't like having someone else's around the place. What a strange idea!

But one good thing had come out of the exchange. He realized he had been going about it all wrong. God bless Nanny, but she had not been right this time. These parties were not the way to find the sort of wife he could live with. The young women were either too silly or too modern. A marriage of convenience. That's what he needed. He wouldn't mind being married if it were genuinely convenient—for both parties, of course. He wanted to live his life as he wished, and his wife could do the same. They could even live in different places. He wanted an heir, but it would all be arranged as a matter of convenience to them both. He did not want his wife to have lovers, and he would not have mistresses because that would inevitably cause problems, which would be very *in*convenient. Yes, a real marriage of convenience, what an excellent notion. There must be a woman somewhere who felt the same. He would put a notice in the papers the next day.

The following morning he sat at his desk and proceeded in his characteristically logical fashion. What did he need in a wife? He wanted someone kind and understanding, like Nanny. Someone intelligent. Someone he could talk to. Then he thought about what his father had said in that very room. Her father had to be a gentleman and she must be a lady. She must give him an heir. So he began a notice:

The Marquess of Hastings is seeking a marriage of convenience with a woman who is kind, understanding and able to talk intelligently. She must be a lady, descended from a gentleman and be able to bear an heir.

Then he remembered. The marriage must be convenient for both of them. What could he give her? He completed the notice:

She will be able to have a life of her own, she need not live with him all the time and the intimate aspects of marriage will only take place when mutually convenient.

He thought again and added:

Neither party will take lovers.

He was going to end the notice when he realized there was one more thing. There was something he had heard all his life. He didn't want to hear it from his wife. He added another sentence:

She must never accuse him of being odd.

Apply in writing to the Marquess of Hastings, Farrell House, Grosvenor Square.

He wrote a note to the editors of *The General Advertiser* telling them to send the bill to his man of business and giving the address. He folded it all into an envelope, poured melted wax to seal it, and pressed it with the signet ring bearing the letter H he had inherited from his father. He then rang for the butler, gave it to him for delivery and sat back with satisfaction. His problems were over.

Chapter Ten

It wasn't very long before the Marquess knew better. The first sign that his plan was not a good one was the constant pulling of the doorbell announcing the arrival of letters. They poured in: five, ten, fifty, a hundred. Jessop the butler, though much younger than the one in Farrell Court, was exhausted by the flow, and finally ordered the senior footman to take his place in the hall. He repaired to his pantry and poured himself a much-needed restorative, then another.

James was at first delighted with the response. It is true he had not expected so many. He would not have believed there could be so many gentlewomen in London looking for a marriage of convenience. It just went to show, he thought. All this talk about poetry and moonlight, and in fact women wanted the same as men: a quiet life with a kind and understanding spouse, and the freedom to do as one wanted.

He was disappointed when he began to read, however. If many of the women who wrote to him considered themselves ladies, not to mention intelligent, they very much mistook the matter. Their mode of self-expression, not to mention their spelling and orthography, shocked him. Surely the flower of British womanhood could do better than this?

14, Shoreditch High Street

My Deer Marquess,

I Sawed yr Notice in the Paper and have Taken The Liberty of Response. My Father is a Gentleman, not as Society mite say It but a Gentleman of Nature. He was a Clerk in a Bank until his Health give Out. He is at Home now under the Feet of my Mamma, for why I am wanting my own Establishment. I can live With you or Apart. Apart mite be Best as I'll be bringin My Jimmy with me, his Dad being gone from the Drink. So you see, I can give you an Heir, either Your Own, or Mine. I likes to Talk and all that. I won't never call you odd, that I can Promisse.

Yrs Truly.

Emmie Thomas (Mrs as was)

The ones that came from obvious radicals like the woman who had spoken to him the other night were even worse. They combined a patent dislike of the male sex with an overweening sense of their own rectitude.

4, Bruton Street

Sir,

(Though I hesitate to use that address to anyone whom I do not know to have earned it),

Your notice in the paper interests me greatly as I see in it the mind of an evolved male, unlike the majority one meets. I and my friends consider ourselves equal to men. We see matrimony as the meeting of minds, not bodies, a union in which a couple may grow in affection through the exchange of ideas, not the subjugation of the marriage bed. I am prepared, however, to do what is necessary to provide you with an heir, however much the mind rejects the distasteful and undignified aspect of it. Having done so, I would expect to live entirely apart, even, I must say, from the child, who can, no doubt, be satisfactorily raised by nannies until it is time to go to school.

> As for never calling you odd, I beg leave to say that I should feel free to call you anything I wish. Complete freedom of expression is essential in a happy partnership.
>
> Yours in equality,
> Mariah Goodsmith (Miss)

As he steadily worked his way through the pile of letters, he soon became expert at recognizing at a glance those he could immediately dismiss. He needed only to read the first sentence. Nevertheless, the process took time and letters continued to pile up.

The second immediately apparent problem was that a number of women, presumably trusting neither their penmanship nor their written powers of persuasion, decided to show up in person at Farrell House. A queue soon formed from the front door down the street, much to the annoyance of pedestrians, deliverymen and, needless to say, the staff of Farrell House. James was amazed when he looked down from his bedroom window on the first day.

The queue of women was attracting no little attention from the carriages and riders going down the street, with the passing gentlemen slowing to a walk to get a good look at the feminine pulchritude there on display. It wasn't every day Grosvenor Square afforded such a sight, and more than one turned his horse to ride back and take in the scene a second time. The effect on traffic is easily imagined, and before long a constable was blowing his whistle, horses were rearing up and it was only luck that prevented a serious accident.

Before James could decide what to do, one candidate managed to get by the butler and the footman. They had no experience of this type of visitor, and felt they could hardly refuse entry to a person coming in answer to the Marquess' own advertisement.

Shown into the drawing room, she was discovered by James prinking her hair in front of the fireplace mirror. The hair in question was of a yellow that did not appear in nature and clashed violently with the puce-colored gown tightly swathing her opulent figure, leaving very little to the imagination.

"Ooh!" she said, coming forward, "Are you the Marquess, then? Well I never! I made sure you'd be some 'orrible old feller 'oo couldn't get a wife 'cept by advertising. But you're a lovely man!"

She approached him as if to take him in her arms, and he was forced to back up until he was against a console table standing next to the wall.

"Don't be afraid, lovey, I won't 'urt yer! Just give us a little kiss!"

Luckily, the bell pull was close at hand and he tugged it. The butler, who must have been right outside the door, came in immediately.

"Miss… er, Miss… is leaving, Jessop," said the Marquess, sidling towards the door with the lady in hot pursuit. "Thank you, Miss…, er… that will be all," he said, and as she reached him by the open door, took her arm and propelled her and the butler through it. He could hear her complaining that 'is lordship didn't even get the chance to know 'er at all, until the front door opened and she was ushered, or pushed, outside.

He waited a moment or two and then went into the hall. "I'm sorry, Jessop," he said. "I had no idea it would come to this. Send them all away. Say written application only. Just keep sending them away."

Having completed this assignment and been subjected to vociferous complaints and not a little jeering, the butler again had to stagger away to his parlor for the sake of his health.

It can easily be imagined that an event of this kind did not long escape the notice of the newspapers. Anything involving a peer of the realm in some sort of scandal was always grist to their mill. The following day articles appeared in most of the papers, together with a reprint of James's original advertisement, or as much of it as they could get away with without infringing copyright laws.

The Marquess was then treated to a visit from his outraged uncle and cousin, who, if they had not seen the reports themselves, soon heard about it from their friends. On the whole, he thought he preferred the visit from the yellow-haired harpy.

"What can have possessed you, James?" bellowed his uncle. "We are laughing stocks of the whole town! Everywhere I go I hear nothing but *a marriage of convenience*. I've never been so embarrassed in my life! You realize you've ruined any chance you had of finding a well-bred girl to marry you now? Not one would touch you with a pair of tongs! I've heard a couple are congratulating themselves on a lucky escape. You might as well start moving your traps out of Farrell Court. Not that I want to live in the damned place, but Eustace is keen."

"Well, yes, of course," tittered his cousin. "With the new baby and another nanny, we need the space."

James clenched his fists and forced himself to breathe slowly. "I still have two weeks," he said as calmly as he could. "Don't move the nanny in yet, Eustace. I should hate to see you have to move her out again. Now, if you'll excuse me, I have letters to read. I'm sure you understand."

And he rang the bell.

"My uncle and cousin are leaving, Jessop," he said. "They can't stay longer."

Chapter Eleven

Elisabeth Maxwell read the newspaper every day after her stepfather had finished with it. She usually found it crumpled on his desk, or sometimes on the floor, and retrieved it, smoothing it out as she went. She carried it up to her room, since the sight of her reading it convinced her stepfather even more that she was the bluestocking he had wasted his money on bringing out.

"There you are, reading again," he would exclaim in annoyance. "I tell you, daughter, no man wants a woman who spends her day with her head in the newspaper! Why don't you learn how to play a pretty tune on the piano upstairs? That's a thing a man would like to see a girl doing! Besides, I paid good blunt to bring the instrument up to snuff, and it sits there untouched."

Thus it was that she saw the report of the disturbance in Grosvenor Square. The reporter had not held back.

The normally sedate air surrounding one of Mayfair's finest neighborhoods was unusually disturbed this morning. It was not the sighting of some rare-plumaged bird that brought forth droves of onlookers, though the gowns and flounced petticoats of the persons lining the linkway in front of the stately home of the Marquess of Hastings were as colorful as in any exotic aviary. For these women had all decked themselves in their very finest to try to dazzle the peer who had advertised for a wife.

He is looking, he says, for a marriage of convenience. He requires only that his spouse be a lady, be kind, intelligent and able to carry on a conversation. Oh, yes. And she must produce an heir, the procreation of the child being, of course, at a moment of mutual convenience. How orderly, and how sophisticated! Of love there is no mention, nor of any softer emotion that might be supposed to smooth the path of marriage.

And yet they came, these women in their Sunday best, hindering pedestrians, disrupting traffic and frightening the horses, to try their hand at winning the prize. To be a Marchioness is something indeed!

One caveat, tucked at the bottom of the notice, may give a wise woman pause, however. She may never call her spouse odd. Yet what else may one call such an advertisement, such requirements, such a suitor? We wish the winner good luck, whoever she may be. She will need it.

Ellie put the newspaper down in astonishment. She was not at all impressed by the reporter's rhetoric or his sarcasm. Here was the answer to her problem! What caught her eye and imprinted itself on her brain was the description of the required wife: a lady, kind and able to carry on a conversation. She was all three, the last to a fault, it had been said. As to producing an heir, she knew nothing about what that entailed, but she was sure she could do whatever was required. Women did it all the time. It couldn't be that hard. But there was no time to think about that now; she must go to Grosvenor Square and join the queue.

She went to her wardrobe and took out her pale blue muslin day dress. Stepping out of the old grey gown she wore around the house, she put it on. Immediately, the color enhanced the bloom in her cheeks and deepened the color of her eyes. She had refurbished a bonnet with blue ribbons and the same small white paper roses she had worn in her hair to her first ball. Having wound her hair on to the top of her head, with just a few strands waving by her face, she put it on.

She looked at herself, and as women always do, focusing on what she considered the least attractive thing about herself: her mousy brown hair. She did not see the intelligent humor in her eyes or the creaminess of her complexion. She made a face at herself. "Well, either he'll like you or he won't," she said out loud to the mirror.

She drew her ivory shawl around her shoulders, pulled on her gloves and snatched up her old reticule. Then, thinking for a moment, she took off her gloves, went back into the wardrobe and took out the smaller, prettier purse her stepfather had given her. Into it she tucked a clean handkerchief, a few coins for the hackney carriage and several of the visiting cards her mother had insisted be printed for her coming out. Drawing her gloves back on as she left the room, she ran lightly down the stairs and out into the street.

When they were poor, her mother and she had not been able to afford her a maid as a chaperone, so she had become entirely accustomed to going out unaccompanied. The question had come up a few times since the marriage to her stepfather, but he did not really want to spend money on another maid, and she did not want the annoyance of someone always around her, so she gladly continued as she was. She quickly found a carriage, inquired the cost of the fare to Grosvenor Square, haggled for a moment and climbed in. A few minutes later, she was let down in front of the residence of the Marquess of Hastings, an address that was by now well known to the London hackney drivers.

It was almost two days since the advertisement had appeared, and the queue of candidates had been firmly dispersed every time it had begun to form. The numbers had been dropping as word spread that no one was getting past the front door, and by now, in the middle of a hot afternoon, even the most stalwart had given up. Ellie was surprised and pleased not to have to wait. She had no idea earlier candidates had been told firmly to go away. The Marquess would see no one.

She tripped up the wide front steps between the stone griffons holding the shield with the *blazon* of the house, and pulled the bell. After a few minutes, the door was opened a crack and Jessop peeped out. He saw a very ladylike young woman, modestly dressed, holding out a visiting card.

"I am Elisabeth Maxwell," she said in a cultivated, well-modulated voice. "I wish to see his lordship, the Marquess."

The butler hesitated. Was this one of the unwanted women, or a different sort of person altogether? He looked at her card. The *Honorable Elisabeth Maxwell*, it read.

"I'm an author," said Ellie. "Of children's books."

An Honorable and a writer of children's books? She couldn't be one of the shameless hussies they had had such difficulties getting rid of, could she? She didn't look or sound like one. She didn't have a maid, which was troubling, but she was clearly a lady. One could always tell. She was probably an acquaintance of the Marquess. Jessop came to a decision.

"Please come in, Miss Maxwell," he led her into the hall and gestured to a seat. "Please wait a few minutes. I will see if his lordship is available."

Chapter Twelve

Silently entering the study, Jessop found the Marquess flicking through the pile of letters on his desk with a look of despair on his face.

"Not one of them!" he said. "Not a single lady amongst them! They all *say* they are, but you can tell from the way they express themselves they're not!"

Jessop dared to say what everyone was thinking. "It may be that a real lady wouldn't respond to an announcement like that, my lord" he said gently. Then he coughed. "But there *is* a lady waiting to see you, sir. A Miss Elisabeth Maxwell. She's an author." He handed James Ellie's card. "I... er, I don't think she's one of the... *others*, my lord."

The Marquess got to his feet, looking at the card. "The Honorable Elisabeth Maxwell? Now where do I know that name from?" he muttered and stood stock still, thinking. Then his brow cleared. "The Temple Of The Muses!" he exclaimed. "Polynesia! Writing a children's book. That's it! I wonder what she wants. Put her in the drawing room, Jessop."

When he entered the drawing room a few minutes later, Miss Maxwell was sitting on one of the small sofas with which the room was amply provided. She stood as he came forward and then said with surprise, "But you're Mr. Farrell, aren't you? I remember you! Are you here to see the Marquess as well?"

"No, he's dead," replied James, thinking she must be referring to his late father.

"Dead? Good heavens!" She felt the wind being taken out of her sails. Her potential husband dead before she even had a chance to meet him! "I'm sorry! It must have been very sudden." She sank back onto the sofa.

"Yes, it was. He broke his neck falling off a horse. It refused at a gate and he went sailing over."

"He was jumping gates in the center of London?" Ellie was puzzled.

"No, of course not, he was at home in the country."

"But weren't all those women waiting to see him? Did they know he wasn't in town?"

"What women?" It was his lordship's turn to be puzzled.

"The women who came in answer to the advertisement."

"But they weren't here to see him. They were here to see me."

"But the advertisement said the Marquess of Hastings." Ellie was beginning to think she had entered an insane asylum. Then suddenly she had a flash of inspiration. "Are *you* the Marquess of Hastings? Now that your father is... no longer with us?"

"Yes, of course. Who did you think I was?" He fixed her with his black stare.

"James Farrell. That's what you told me."

"I *am* James Farrell, Sixth Marquess of Hastings. Only I wasn't when I met you. The Marquess, I mean. My father was still alive then."

Elisabeth laughed with relief. "I'm glad we cleared that up! I began to think I was going mad! Oh, I'm sorry—I shouldn't be laughing. I'm sorry to hear about your father's death. Mine died too—about two years ago. I miss him dreadfully."

The Marquess's expression had lightened when Ellie laughed, and he gave a bark of laughter now, too. "I wish I could say the same. Mine wasn't a bad father, but he did like his own way, and I'm afraid we didn't often see eye to eye."

They were both silent for a moment, thinking about their fathers, she with love, he with something closer to dislike.

Then, remembering the manners instilled into him from the earliest age, his lordship turned to his visitor and said, "But how may I be of service to you, Miss Maxwell?"

Ellie drew in her breath. Didn't this strange man know she was here in answer to the advertisement? How embarrassing! How was she to tell him she wanted to marry him?

She was sure she was blushing. "I... I read about your advertisement in the newspaper. I didn't see the original notice. About wanting a... wanting a wife, I mean."

"Yes, I have been trying to find a wife. It's been very difficult. You see...," said James, then he suddenly realized what she meant. He leaped to his feet, a great smile on his face. "You mean *you* want to marry me? By all that's wonderful! I knew there had to be at least one lady in London who would understand! Miss Maxwell! You're perfect! Let's get married tomorrow!"

His joy was so plain, Ellie forgot her embarrassment. "But my lord, why are you in such a hurry? Don't you think it would be a good idea for us to be betrothed first? To get to know each other a little? After all, we may not suit."

"No time for that. Got to be married by the end of next week. Of course we'll suit. It doesn't really matter, anyway. It will be a marriage of convenience. I'll leave you alone and you'll leave me alone. I've just got to be married, that's the thing. I'll ask Jessop if he knows what to do. Butlers always know everything."

He strode rapidly out of the drawing room.

Ellie sat there with her mouth open. Whatever she had expected, it wasn't this. She felt as if she were in some kind of dream, or even nightmare. She found she was gripping the handles of her reticule so hard her knuckles were white. She forced herself to calm down. Could this be true? Was she *really* going to be married to this odd man? No, she mustn't call him odd. Actually, he was quite nice. Wonderful manners. And he *had* said it would be a marriage of convenience; they wouldn't even live together. But that was the point. She didn't want to stay at home. Where *would* she live? Here?

She looked around the elegant drawing room with its silk-covered furnishings, its lofty ceiling with large chandeliers at each end suspended from plaster rosettes, the pale yellow walls topped with a white frieze, the handsome fireplace, the Aubusson rugs, the large, ornately-framed oil paintings at intervals around the room. It was very beautiful, and it was very quiet. A clock ticked sonorously at one end, and the sound of the traffic outside was muffled by the pale blue heavy velvet curtains. Could she possibly call this *home*?

It was a little while before the Marquess came back into the room, long enough for Ellie to begin to feel distinctly uneasy. Perhaps it was all an elaborate hoax, or some sort of joke. But when he came in, he was smiling and rubbing his hands together. "I knew Jessop would be able to tell me. We have to have a special license, apparently, from a bishop. Luckily, he says I know one. Or at least, m'father knew one. At school together. I've just dashed off a note asking to see him tomorrow. Then we can get married the day after, all right and tight. Just need to find a vicar, but the bishop's bound to know one. They're all part of the same business, after all."

"But my lord, there are things we do need to discuss. Just a little. You talk about living apart. I do not wish to continue living with my mother and stepfather. Where would I live, and, if you don't mind my indelicate question, what would I live on?"

"You can stay here if you want to." He looked around nonchalantly, "And there will be settlements, of course. I believe my mother had money that goes to the next Marchioness. That will all get sorted out. Our solicitor will see to it. But I shan't be staying here. Soon as we're married, I'm off to Maylands."

"Maylands?"

"Our place in the country. Middlesex. Nice old pile. My real home. You can come there if you want, but don't expect to see much of me. I've got a lot to do."

"Is it a farm?"

"Of course it's a farm! A very large farm. And I've been improving the land to raise very large cattle. I told you that when I met you before. Don't you remember?" He stared at her again.

Ellie was disconcerted by the stare, but she was beginning to understand he only stared like that when a question caught his interest. So she stared right back. "Yes, I do remember," she said and smiled.

He smiled back, a beautiful, warm smile that transformed his face. "Good," he said. "Then you'll understand I have to get back to it. It's nearly harvest time. I want to check the yields. It's very important."

"Yes, I can see that. If you don't mind I should like to come to Maylands, too." She was thinking rapidly. "Perhaps I can write a children's book about living on a farm. I'm sure most town-bred children have no idea where milk comes from."

"Excellent! You shall have your work, and I shall have mine. We need not get in each other's way at all. Now, Miss Maxwell…"

She interrupted. "I think perhaps you should call me Elisabeth or Ellie, if we are to be married. May I call you James?"

"Of course." He smiled at her again. "Now, Elisabeth, if you don't object, I shall see you out. I have a large number of letters to write. To begin with, I must answer all the women who wrote to me."

"How many are there?"

"About two hundred."

"Good gracious! You can't be expected to write two hundred letters!" cried Ellie. "It would take ages! I have an idea. Why don't you place a notice in the newspaper to thank all the candidates at once and say you have found a suitable lady?"

His face lit up. "That is a capital notion! I say, Miss Max… Elisabeth, you are clever! Do you think I should give your name?"

"Heavens no!" said Ellie. "I might have droves of women wanting to tear my hair out!"

"Why?"

"Because I have ruined their chances, of course."

"But none of them had a chance," said James seriously. "I couldn't have chosen one of them."

Ellie laughed. "Now, that is not very gallant, sir! You should have told me I faced stiff competition but won because of my superior charms."

"Should I?" he looked puzzled. "But that would not be the truth. Nanny taught me to always tell the truth." He fixed his gaze on her.

"And so you should, for things that matter, but surely you've heard of a white lie? If you tell me I've beaten out the competition, it hurts no one and is a compliment to me."

"But do you want me to give you a compliment that's a lie? That seems very strange." He was absolutely serious.

"But I wouldn't know it was a lie," responded Elisabeth. Then, looking at the puzzled expression that filled his eyes, she realized he really didn't understand, and laughed kindly.

"But no matter! I should not expect gallantry, after all. This is more of a business matter, I collect. Please tell me, my lord, what should I do now? May I tell my family about our... I was going to say, engagement, but it isn't really, is it?"

"No, I suppose not. But I can tell you, Miss Maxwell, Elisabeth, that we shall be married as soon as I can obtain a license. I shall send you a note about the final arrangements."

"You will find my direction at the bottom of my card. Would you like another, in case you lose it?"

"I never lose things," said James firmly. "But perhaps I'd better have another card in case I need to give it to someone else." A thought struck him. "Of course, I shall have to inform Sanderson. He's the family solicitor. He will have to draw up papers. The settlements, and so on. I'll let you know. Now, if you don't mind, I'll see you out."

Chapter Thirteen

After being ushered out of Farrell House, Ellie rode home in a daze. Was it really true? Was she going to marry the Marquess of Hastings? She reviewed the extraordinary interview and could find nothing in it that proved it wasn't. Besides, it was clear his lordship—James, she must get used to that—did not know how to tell a lie. Besides, what had she expected? She had acted on impulse when she had run out and jumped into a hackney that afternoon but she knew the man was looking for a wife. Hadn't she wanted him to choose her? Well, he had.

Apparently he thought she was better than the others. More than that, he had called her *perfect*. She smiled to herself. He really was quite sweet in an odd way. No, she really must stop even thinking him odd. After all, she told herself, being married to him couldn't be any worse than living with her stepfather. He had said she would hardly see him. That did sound perfect. No one to criticize her reticule or her appearance in general, no one to complain if she read the newspaper, no one to make stupid statements as pompously as if they were handed down with the Ten Commandments. Under the conditions the Marquess had outlined, she felt marriage would be quite bearable. Then she thought: *Marquess*! She would be the Marchioness, and have settlements, whatever they were! She laughed out loud. How funny!

When it appeared in the papers, the notice that the Marquess of Hastings had found a suitable candidate for a wife caused almost as much uproar as the one announcing his search. To be sure, there were no lines outside his front door, but Ellie was right. It was as well the women who had been rejected didn't know her name.

They openly criticized her, whoever she was. "No better than she should be," was their frequent opinion, with "brazen hussy" coming a close second.

In the clubs and around the dinner tables of the *ton* it was a chief topic of gossip and speculation. "I'd like to see this *lady* who can talk intelligently and doesn't find him odd," said those who knew him. "Wherever did he find her?"

No one came forward as the blushing winner of the race, and no one had any idea who she could be.

James's uncle and cousin were amongst the first at his door to demand an explanation. Cousin Eustace was furious.

"In my opinion, it's all a hum," he said. "You just don't want me at Maylands. I won't believe in this woman till I see her."

"Come to the wedding if you like," said James carelessly. "Then you can see her." He didn't care who came and who didn't, so long as it took place.

He and Elisabeth were not, of course, married the very next day. He had been amazed how much there was to arrange. He had obtained a special license fairly easily, but it had taken time to find a church for the service. That had not been so easy, but in the end he found a vicar who was thrilled at the idea of a Marquess being married in his church. The faded spinsters who worked tirelessly to maintain both the premises and him (for he was unmarried), were already polishing the brasses and bringing in armfuls of flowers.

"You mean you're not sending invitations?"

"No. No time. Anyway, it will be a very quiet wedding. Only family."

"Your father wouldn't have liked it," said his uncle censoriously. "The head of the family being married in an out of the way place with no witnesses."

"It's not out of the way. It's in Mayfair. There will be witnesses. Nanny is coming up from Maylands and Eliz... my future wife's godmother will do the honors."

"Nanny? You don't mean your old nanny is going to be a witness?"

"Certainly I do. She deserves it more than anyone. And if my father wouldn't have liked it, he shouldn't have put that ridiculous provision in his Will."

"Very poor, I call it," grumbled Eustace. Then he cheered himself with a thought. "Perhaps she won't produce an heir."

James thought about that for a moment, considering Elisabeth as he might have a heifer he intended to purchase. "She is a fine, healthy woman," he said at last. "I see no reason why she shouldn't."

"If it's convenient," sneered his cousin.

"Quite," said the Marquess, and left the room.

Chapter Fourteen

Elisabeth had decided she would wait until she heard from her intended before saying anything to her mother and stepfather. The whole thing was so unbelievable, she was still half afraid it would still turn out to be a sham, or a joke, or even a wager between young men of the *ton*. She had heard they would bet on anything. Somehow, thinking of James's dark gaze and his reaction to telling a lie, she didn't think so. Still, best be safe.

In the event, it was more than two days before she heard from him, enough time for her to convince herself the whole thing had, indeed, been unreal. But on the morning of the third day she received an epistle, written in a remarkably fine hand.

Farrell House
Grosvenor Square, London

Dear Miss Maxwell,

You may wonder at my delay in sending you this promised note. I have been working on the details of our marriage since we last spoke, but it has taken longer than I anticipated.

I have now obtained a special marriage license from the bishop. He was more difficult to deal with than I had imagined, and what I had thought would be an interview of a few minutes lasted over an hour. He inquired most presumptuously into my private affairs, as so I told him. For a moment it seemed as if he might refuse the license, but then I remembered my father saying that bishops would do anything if one promised enough money. This proved, indeed to be the case. When I asked whether there was an opportunity for me to donate to some cause or other, the thing was soon arranged.

While he was able to supply me with the names of churches under his control, he could not, however, tell me at which one the ceremony might be held. He said I would have to speak to the vicar concerned. I informed him that if any of the people in my employ could not be told what to do, they would not long remain in my employ, but he failed to see the parallel.

Armed with the list of churches he gave me, I spent the rest of the day and the next visiting them. It is not an exercise I would wish to repeat. I am tempted to write to the Bishop of London and complain about the laziness and ineffectiveness of most of the clergy in London. They could not be disturbed, they were at table, they were from home, they were, in a word, doing anything other than seeing to the happiness of their flocks. It finally occurred to me I might have better luck sending in my card as the Marquess of Hastings rather than calling myself simply James Farrell. I had at first decided not to use the title, not wanting word to be spread abroad that the House of Hastings had to stoop to begging for a church for the matrimony of its Marquess.

The very first time I had the groom take in my card, the welcome I received was fulsome in the extreme. My request was immediately granted, with the result we are to be wed at the Grosvenor Chapel on South Audley Street at half past eleven on Thursday (two days hence). It is a little place with a quite fine organ (at least, so the vicar tells me). He asked me about music, and I told him do to whatever is suitable. He seemed delighted to have a member of the aristocracy married in his church. I don't know much about these *matters, but I believe that vicars are even worse paid than rectors. No doubt my father's dictum about bishops applies here as well. I shall have Sanderson look into it.*

Talking of Sanderson brings me to my last point. He will attend us here at Farrell House this afternoon at two. I shall send a carriage to convey you here.

Please accept my expression of deepest respect,
James Farrell

Ellie did not know whether to be amused or annoyed by this letter. His lordship had obviously worked hard to make the arrangements, but it had not occurred to him that she might like a say in where she was to be wed. Nor had he asked whether that afternoon was convenient to meet the solicitor. But of course it was. She had deliberately cried off all other engagements, even refusing to go shopping with her mother because she wanted to be home if the promised note arrived.

At lunch she calmly told her mother and stepfather she had an engagement that afternoon. They were accustomed to her leaving the house without much explanation, so made no comment. They did not see the emblazoned carriage when it arrived. Ellie had been watching for it and slipped out of the house before the groom rang the bell. Having worn her blue day dress on the previous occasion, she had put on the pale pink sprigged muslin and quickly replaced the blue ribbon on her bonnet with a pink one. The pink really did bring a bloom to her cheek and, her color naturally heightened by the suppressed excitement in her bosom, she looked pretty.

That was the solicitor's first thought when she was shown into the drawing room at Farrell House. He had arrived a few minutes early and was interrogating the Marquess about his intended nuptials as only an old family retainer might.

"Are you sure, my lord, you are not making a mistake?" he had just been saying. "To be wed with barely any acquaintance was common in the last century, but these days we believe young couples should know each other better."

"Yes, I'm sure," said James. "She was the only one who was any good, in any case."

"As to that, sir," the solicitor looked pained, "a notice in the newspaper was… well, let us just say, your late father would not have approved."

"He would have no one to blame but himself. It was all his fault. Anyway, it's done. I'm getting married on Thursday and there's an end to it."

At that point, Jessop ushered in Elisabeth, and both men rose. Ellie thought the solicitor looked exactly as she had expected: desiccated and grey. Sanderson, however, was pleasantly surprised. The future Marchioness looked ladylike and pretty, not at all what he had expected. He had rather thought the Marquess would be trapped by an opera-singer. James was just pleased she had turned up on time. He had heard from a number of his friends that females were likely to be late because of changing their gowns or bonnets at the last moment, and had actually wondered whether he should set the time for her arrival ahead of Sanderson.

The discussion centered almost entirely upon the mysterious settlements. It seemed that besides the legacy of the previous Marchioness, of which Ellie was to enjoy the interest paid quarterly, and which she thought very generous, she was also to receive an allowance from her husband. The solicitor had worked this out based upon the allowance given to the previous Lady Hastings, allowing for inflation of over twenty years. She at first thought that quarterly payment was the annual total and when she realized her mistake, she blinked.

"Good gracious!" she exclaimed. "That seems a very great deal of money!"

"I think you will find it commensurate with the allowances of other ladies of your future rank," said Mr. Sanderson gravely. "You will have expenses, particularly in the matter of raiment, far greater than you have hitherto experienced."

He looked at her simple muslin dress. It was pretty, no doubt, all very well for an unmarried girl of no consequence, but for the Marchioness of Hastings, it would not do, oh dear me, no.

"But I shall be living mostly in the country!" she said, "I shall not need anything very fine!"

"Even in the country, Miss Maxwell," replied the solicitor firmly, "you will find you have a standard to maintain."

Ellie said nothing, but wondered how she was to know what those standards were and to whom she should go to achieve them. She wondered if her Mama's *modiste* would know. It was true she had already realized her two new day dresses were not nearly enough. Her future husband had now seen both of them and she had known him less than a week. Not that he seemed to have noticed. In any case, there was no time to have anything made.

As he tucked the papers into a large folder emblazoned with a gold letter H, the solicitor said, "With your permission, sir, I shall attend the wedding. At that point I shall give the Marchioness," and he bowed in Ellie's direction, "a cash advance on her allowance. Then for her future needs she may apply to Hoare's, where your own accounts, as you know, are held."

Receiving an affirmative nod from the Marquess, he bowed and took his leave.

Elle felt compelled to explain something to her future husband. "James, I must tell you time is too short for me to obtain a new gown for the wedding. I shall have to wear one I already own. I hope that will be satisfactory."

He looked surprised. "But naturally it will be satisfactory," he said. "To tell you the truth, I hadn't given any thought to the question of wedding garments. We shall both of us wear whatever we have. It is of no importance, after all."

Ellie sat there, reflecting that her wedding clothes were a thought that generally occupied a maiden's mind for months, and sometimes, years. And Sanderson had talked about *standards*. James seemed to notice nothing and began to rise, presumably to see her to the door.

She rose too, but asked, "Shall we leave immediately for Maylands? No... er, wedding breakfast or anything?"

"Certainly we shall. I have no desire to stay in London a minute longer than necessary. I've got an enormous amount to do on the estate. Harvesting is beginning. If we leave the chapel by half past twelve, we should be at Maylands before three, allowing a stop to rest the horses. A wedding breakfast? No, we can have a luncheon when we stop. I'll send them a note now."

"But what about our guests?"

"Who?"

"Your nanny and my godmother Lady Penhale who are witnesses, my mother and stepfather, Mr. Sanderson, and you must have *some* family members who will be there, don't you?"

"Only my uncle and cousin. They'll probably come. I said they could if they wanted."

"Don't they have wives?"

"God, yes. My aunt Honoria." He shuddered. "And Eustace's wife Penelope. Do you think they'll come too?"

"Yes, of course! You are the head of the family, are you not? It would be very remiss of them to neglect your wedding."

The Marquess sighed. "Well, I'm not staying here to entertain a single one of them. Nanny will come back with us in the carriage, so she can have nuncheon with us. The rest can just go home."

"But you are the Marquess," she said. " I think for the sake of the family name, you need to do a little more than that. Perhaps you could bespeak a luncheon for them at Grillon's. We need not go, if you prefer not to, but it would be shabby to send them off home with nothing. And have you considered the staff here and at Farrell Court? I believe it is customary to give them a *douceur* on the occasion of the wedding of an important family member."

James looked at her with exasperation. "Good Lord," he exclaimed. "All I wish to do is get married and go home. What more must I do?"

"Why don't you call in Jessop and ask his advice?" she replied. "You said yourself butlers know everything."

James looked at her with gratitude. "Good idea," he said, and went to ring the bell.

Ellie was making her way to the door, when she stopped. "James," she asked suddenly, "why do we have to be married so quickly?"

"Didn't I tell you?" he answered. "It's because my father's Will stipulated that if I don't marry within four months, I lose an important part of Maylands."

"And you would do anything to keep it all, I collect?" she responded quietly.

"Yes. It means everything to me." He looked at her with his dark gaze.

So, that was it, thought Miss Maxwell. He's marrying you to save the thing he loves most in the world. That's why what we wear at the wedding, or who comes, or how it is celebrated, is of no importance. It's the land he wants. He doesn't really want you at all. Even though she knew love had nothing to do with their marriage, the thought gave her a sudden pang.

"I shall send a carriage for you at eleven o'clock on Thursday morning to convey you to the chapel, " said James, politely walking her into the hall. "You won't be late, will you?" He looked at her anxiously, remembering the stories about the gowns and bonnets.

"Of course not," Ellie replied.

"You know I shall be leaving for Maylands directly after the wedding," he reminded her. "Even if there is a wedding breakfast. If you wish to come with me, you'd better bring whatever you need to the chapel."

"Yes."

There didn't seem much more to say.

Chapter Fifteen

For the second time after leaving her intended, Ellie rode home with her head in a whirl, not because she wasn't sure what was happening, but because she was. The settlements had been explained; the marriage was going to take place. She knew that on Thursday she was leaving her home and going to live for the rest of her life with a virtual stranger.

There had been nothing today of the sweetness in her future husband's nature apparent when she saw him last. Nothing of that smile. Today he had been all business. She shook herself. Of course he had; they had been talking to the solicitor, or rather, he had been talking to them. But one thing was abundantly clear. The wedding was just a piece of business to be concluded before he could do what he really wanted: get back to Maylands and his farming.

When she arrived home, Ellie went to her mother's room, where she found her sewing a torn flounce on a gown.

"Mama," she said, sitting down by her feet, "I have something to tell you that will surprise you very much." She proceeded to tell her the whole extraordinary story, omitting, however, the details of the marriage of convenience. "And now on Thursday," she concluded, "I am to leave you and go to live in Middlesex with my new husband."

Beneath her fragile and self-effacing exterior, like most mothers, Mrs. Brownlow had a core of steel where her child was concerned. The difficulty of settling her daughter appropriately with the very limited means available to her had been one of the chief factors that had led her to accept Mr. Brownlow. She knew she would never love him as she had loved Ellie's father, but thought that both her and her daughter's future would be more comfortable with him than without. But it was now clear that Ellie could never be happy in the same house as her stepfather. They chafed each other constantly. Mrs. Brownlow understood her daughter's wanting to leave, but also knew it was a frightening prospect to live as a spinster with no money. So not for a moment did she argue with her daughter's decision to marry, no matter how unconventional the whole affair appeared. Only one aspect of the matter caused her to burst into tears. "Leave me?" she cried. "Oh, Ellie! I couldn't bear it!"

"But Mama, you must have known that whenever I married I should have to leave you!"

Acknowledging this to be true, Mrs. Brownlow dried her eyes and resolutely looked on the bright side. Her daughter would be well married. She would have a title. And she hadn't said she disliked the man. It would work out. Many a woman had married for security rather than love, after all. She had done so herself. But then a most significant issue struck her.

"Thursday! But your wedding gown!"

"I am not to have a wedding gown."

"No gown?"

"No, but that doesn't worry me as much as the fact that I shall be going into the country for an indefinite period with nothing suitable to wear! And the solicitor said I shall have a standard to maintain. How can I, when I don't even know what that means?"

Her tears now completely forgotten, her mother bustled from her chair and rang the bell for her dresser. "We must see Hélène immediately!"

Her dresser had been with her for many years, even when her wages had been reduced to nearly nothing. She could be trusted absolutely. She was sent with a note to the *modiste*, asking her to come as soon as possible that afternoon to the Brownlow residence. Her services were needed for a most urgent matter.

The result was that by five o'clock the dressmaker was fully apprised of the enormity of the problem. Miss Ellie was to marry a Marquess, albeit a very unconventional one, and was to leave immediately to live in the country. Mrs. Brownlow would not hear of her daughter being married without a suitable dress. Members of the Marquess's family were bound to be at the wedding and it was unthinkable they should think her daughter a nobody from nowhere. She would be as richly gowned as they could manage. The *modiste* was to produce it. Then, as quickly as possible, she was to make up a suitable wardrobe for a county gentlewoman.

"I shall have money to pay for it all on the day of my wedding," said Ellie. "Mr. Sanderson said so. In fact, Mama, he said I should have," she whispered the enormous sum , "… a *quarter*!"

Her Mama was startled. Ellie was to be a wealthy woman. "In that case, I have no hesitation in telling you, Hélène," she announced to the *modiste*, that we will pay you any sum you name to produce a suitable wedding gown by this time tomorrow. Then you may take a week or so to produce as many gowns as you think appropriate for the country. I imagine we are talking woolen ensembles that may be used while walking in county lanes or riding in gigs, that sort of thing. And Ellie will need two or three more day gowns. You have her measurements, and I trust your judgement. When they are ready, the items may be sent into Middlesex. We will furnish you with the direction in due course. You will be paid as soon as my daughter is the Marchioness."

It was a testimony to her love of her daughter that Ellie's mother never once thought of a gown for herself.

The *modiste*, who had only ever had penny-pinching clients, was filled with enthusiasm. She left the house thinking that here, at last, was the possibility of achieving her dream: to dress a true member of the *ton*. She would do what they asked or burst in the attempt!

When Mr. Brownlow was finally convinced his step daughter was to marry a Marquess, and it wasn't all a hum, as he suspected, his reaction was not unlike his wife's. Tears came to his eyes. In his case, it was not that he would miss Ellie, but that he saw himself hobnobbing on equal terms with members of the aristocracy, sitting at his son-in-law's table, offering advice, being regarded as a valuable family member. The money he had spent on bringing Elisabeth out was now seen as a wise investment.

Judging the moment ripe, his wife said, "I'm sure you will not object, my dear, to giving me a little extra to buy some essentials for our dear Elisabeth. You will not wish her to take up her position as Marchioness at her country estate with nothing but that old bonnet she always wears, and no boots to speak of."

Mr. Brownlow heard nothing after the words *Marchioness at her country estate* and absently nodded, his mind full of visions of riding to hounds and quaffing stirrup cups with the local gentry.

The next day, therefore, Ellie and her mother indulged in another orgy of buying: boots for muddy lanes, shoes for walking around the grounds in fine weather, slippers for indoors; a new cloak in grey herringbone superfine with a blue silk lining; a jaunty carriage bonnet in pale grey felt with a blue feather to match the cloak lining, and an ivory poke bonnet with interchangeable colored ribbons for mild afternoons. Gloves, stockings, new underwear and nightgowns completed the purchases.

"Good underwear and nightgowns are essential," declared Mrs. Brownlow. "The maids know before anyone who is a lady and who is not. One must have items of excellent quality and restrained design. What one hears about purple silk petticoats does not bear repeating!"

Since Ellie had never heard of purple silk petticoats at all, she was intrigued, but all her mother would say was, "*not* a thing any *lady* would wear!"

So the items they purchased were of fine cotton lawn, with a delicate edging of *broderie anglaise*, a little staid, perhaps, but of the first quality.

The following day towards evening, Hélène reappeared with a large box which, when opened, revealed a long-sleeved, ivory silk wedding gown. It looked like a ribbon of cream as she held it up for inspection. A short train of point d'Alençon lace fell from the shoulders in the back and it had a band of the same lace inset beneath the bosom.

"The lace is a little dear, Madam," confessed the *modiste*, "but the gown is otherwise very simple. The beauty is all in the cut. I thought that since other members of the groom's family are sure to be there, you would not wish to appear in any way *mean*." This exactly accorded with Mrs. Brownlow's ideas and she nodded enthusiastically. Any possible doubts disappeared the minute Ellie put the gown on. It fitted her slim figure to perfection, the train falling gracefully behind her. She was transformed.

"The gown is a simpler version of that worn by Princess Charlotte," said Hélène. "Hers had a lace overdress, but for Miss Ellie, I was sure a plain but well-cut gown with just the lace train would be best. I think, too, a wreath of flowers rather than a veil. I understand the... er, groom might not be dressed in wedding attire, and we do not wish Miss Elisabeth to appear... well, overdressed. I have therefore taken the liberty..."

And she produced a pretty crown fashioned of ivory and blue roses which she placed on Ellie's head.

"Perfect," declared the proud Mama. "Ellie, you look wonderful. And you know," she added, her years of making do on a very small clothing budget coming to the fore, "you will only have to remove the lace train for the dress to be converted into a simple dinner gown. With your embroidered shawl it will be perfect."

"I thought of that, Madam, and attached it with some tiny hooks. Look," replied the *modiste,* equally accustomed to thrift. "The length of lace may be used for an overskirt, perhaps, at a future date."

"I doubt I shall need either silk dinner gowns or lace overskirts in the country," laughed Ellie, touched nonetheless by both of the older women's solicitude.

"Then perhaps a Christening gown?" suggested Hélène, "Though I daresay these great families have heirlooms they use on such occasions."

Ellie blanched at the idea of a christening gown. Anxiety suddenly gripped her heart. To use such a thing, one would have to have a child. His lordship had put in the advertisement that his wife was to produce an heir, but the matter had never been mentioned again. She knew nothing of these things. Would Mama tell her the secrets tonight? This was an aspect of the affair she had resolutely pushed to the back of her mind. She lifted her head to her reflection in the mirror and a white, frightened face looked back at her.

Chapter Sixteen

Ellie's mother did indeed have a talk with her daughter that night as she sat for the last time as a girl in her narrow bed. It was not, however, especially illuminating or reassuring.

"You must submit to your husband willingly, my dear," she said as a preamble. "He's a gentleman and you said he was kind, didn't you?"

"Yes," agreed her daughter. "I think so. But what will he want to do?"

Her mother became flustered. "Well, he will want to lie with you and... be one with you," is all she was able to say.

"Be *one*? What does that mean? How?"

"You'll see. It won't take long. It may seem... er, disagreeable at first, but the time will come when you may well enjoy it."

Mrs. Brownlow remembered with a fond smile the intimate moments with Ellie's father, once she had become accustomed to it. Her present husband was more of a trial, with his loud laugh and clumsiness, but fortunately their marital relations were usually over almost before she realized they had begun.

Ellie saw the small smile and was reassured. "But...," she began.

"Don't worry, Ellie, dear. You only need to follow your husband's lead. You will find it will all be quite natural. Now try to get some sleep. You'll have a long day tomorrow."

Needless to say, Ellie lay awake far into the night, fearful that she had made a terrible mistake in agreeing to marry this odd man, fearful of leaving behind everything she had ever known and most of all fearful of this new *being one*. Her mother had smiled when she spoke of it, and said she might well enjoy it, but what exactly was *it*? She fell at last into a restless sleep to be awoken by the maid at nine o'clock with the breakfast tray.

That was the last peaceful moment of the morning. Mrs. Brownlow insisted she prepare for married life by taking a bath. This was usually not more than a weekly event, and Ellie had bathed only four days before, but now all was a-bustle as the maids brought the copper tub up to her room, followed by jugs of hot water, which her mother perfumed with a few drops of her precious rose oil.

Then came the donning of her undergarments: a fine lawn chemise and petticoat. Ellie had never worn a corset and refused to have her mother buy one for the wedding.

"At least let me be comfortable, Mama!" she had exclaimed. "It's bad enough having to appear like a lamb to the slaughter before as many of his lordship's family who show up, without feeling like a trussed turkey into the bargain!"

It was true her breasts were firm enough without boning to hold them up, and her slim waist scarcely needed making any narrower. She then slipped on her silk stockings with the delicate new garters. But before putting on her wedding dress, she donned the first peignoir she had ever owned: a shiny silk garment especially intended, she had learned, to wear when combing one's hair. Wearing this delicious confection, she allowed Mama's dresser to brush her hair up into a topknot, with a few strands left over her ears, and fasten the wreath of roses onto her head. The hanging locks of hair were still a little damp from the steam of the bath, and began to curl as they dried. The whole effect was very pretty, but all Ellie could see as she looked into the mirror were the shadows from lack of sleep and the anxiety in her eyes.

Then she put the last items into her trunk. She had packed just about everything she owned the night before. Now she added her toothbrush, brush and comb and the peignoir, which lay next to her boringly prosaic everyday nightie and dressing gown like a jewel next to a plate of potatoes. Finally, she stepped into the wedding gown held out for her, and allowed herself to be buttoned up.

"Oh, Miss Elisabeth, you look a picture!" cried the dresser, a sentiment echoed by her mother.

"If only your dear Papa could have seen you on your wedding day!" she said, tears in her eyes.

Leaving the trunk to be carried into the hall by the footmen, Ellie went down the stairs to see the whole household standing in the hall. Everyone exclaimed at how pretty she looked and showered her with good wishes. Her stepfather, his chest puffed with pride, accompanied her and her mother to the waiting carriage. There it stood, shining in black ebony picked out with gold, its doors emblazoned with the Hastings crest, and pulled by a pair of matched black horses. The late Marquess had had a fine taste in carriages. There was a slight delay as the trunk was fastened to the back, and then they were off to the Grosvenor Chapel on South Audley Street.

To the bridegroom, standing in the chapel with his best man, an old school friend called in at the last minute because James had forgotten the need for one, the sound of the carriage arriving was an enormous relief. He had been haunted all night by the fear that Miss Maxwell would arrive late, or not at all.

Chapter Seventeen

The Vicar had not been exaggerating when he boasted of the excellence of the organ in the little chapel. And since he had been given a free hand in the choice of music, he and the organist had chosen their favorite pieces. As Elisabeth walked down the aisle on the arm of her stepfather, the glorious *Trumpet Voluntary* filled the nave and flew up to the dome. Until she actually walked through the church doors, the wedding had seemed like a dream. But the soaring and solemnly joyful music finally convinced her of its reality. She lifted her head and walked firmly to meet her future husband.

The congregation only numbered about fifteen people, most of them from the groom's family. They had received a little notice; Ellie's none at all. All heads turned towards her and the members of the groom's family drew in its collective breath. The future Marchioness was a pretty, even beautiful, woman, dressed simply but expensively and with great taste. She certainly looked the part. How had James pulled it off? They would have bet against it. But he had found not only a suitable lady, but one who would be an ornament to the family. Most of them were glad for James's sake. He was odd, to be sure, but he was a good man. Cousin Eustace was livid. His dreams of inheriting Maylands evaporated. Only Nanny was filled with joy. She knew her boy could do it.

James himself looked remarkably handsome. His valet and butler between them had convinced him of the need to appear better turned out than usual. He had grudgingly submitted to having his hair cut and his nails manicured. The thought of having a new coat never crossed his mind. Indeed it would have been impossible, for Weston was his tailor, as he had been his father's before him. That gentleman was far too well-known and busy with lofty clients to consider dropping everything for a man who wore his clothing with such a deplorable lack of care.

So they brushed up the best coat and pantaloons they could find, had the laundry maids wash, starch and iron his shirt with care, and the valet pleaded with his master to sit still while he arranged his neckcloth to a nicety. He fastened it with an emerald pin that had belonged to the late Marquess, then stood back and declared it very fine. James's only contribution was the sour remark that it made his damned head feel like a cabbage on a folded napkin. It remained only to make him wear the Hessians his father had forced him to buy, but which he usually eschewed in favor of his top boots. These had been polished to a glassy shine by the application of wax softened with champagne. The Marquess submitted to the discomfort of having them pulled on, saying only that as soon as they got to Maylands he would put them away and never wear them again. So when Elisabeth beheld her husband-to-be she was pleasantly surprised, and when they stood together they were a handsome couple.

The service was beautiful. The ancient words with which the bride and groom plight each other the troth to cleave together in sickness and in health, for richer, for poorer until death do them part, are impossible to pronounce without solemnity, and this occasion was no exception. James spoke out loudly and firmly, his dark gaze fixed on her from beginning to end. Ellie did the same. To her delight, when the time came, a lovely heavy gold ring was placed on her finger. She wondered where it had come from. But she reckoned without Sanderson. He and his father and his father's father before him had been lawyers to the Marquess of Hastings for nearly a hundred years. They knew where everything was. Sanderson had written a note to his lordship reminding him to remove the wedding ring from the bank vault where it was kept with the rest of the family jewelry and important papers. Perhaps her future ladyship would like to visit the vault after the wedding and choose such of the other jewels as she might like to wear? James had retrieved the wedding ring, but barely glanced at the rest. Why on earth would anyone want any of that stuff in the country?

When the exchange of vows was done, Ellie's godmother and James's nanny, leaning heavily on the groom's arm, went to sign the register. There were a number of raised eyebrows at this departure from convention, but the groom smiled down at the old lady so lovingly that Ellie's heart filled. Afterwards, as the organist filled the little chapel with his own arrangement of *Jesu, Joy Of Man's Desiring*, James smiled at her too, relief patent in his eyes. She smiled back and they walked up the aisle as man and wife.

It was lucky that Nanny was of limited mobility, and moved slowly, for while James went back into the church to fetch her, Ellie had time to have a word with her mother and Lady Penhale. It seemed that the Marquess had taken her advice about a wedding breakfast. Mrs. Brownlow said one of the gentlemen had announced there was to be a gathering at Grillon's.

"We'll see you there," said her mother gaily. She had been worried that her gown had not been a new one, but was reassured when she saw that none of the other women looked as if they had a new one either. "We can't wait to meet the Marquess!"

"I'm sorry, Mama, but James wants to leave immediately for Middlesex. He's very anxious to get back to his estates."

"What? Immediately?" cried her mother. "I knew you were going into the country, but I had no idea it would be right away!"

"Not going to your own wedding breakfast? How very strange!" said Lady Penhale. "We haven't even met the Marquess yet!"

"He isn't really interested in... in that sort of thing," said Ellie. "He's rather... different."

Having deposited Nanny in the carriage, James arrived just at that moment and was presented to the ladies. He made a very correct bow and said he was at their service.

This was, of course, merely a polite form of words for he had no sooner said it than he added earnestly, "We must leave you now. I've been gone more than three months and there is so much to do."

"We had hoped to get to know you a little, my lord," said Mrs. Brownlow. "I hope we'll see you back in London soon."

"Oh, I shouldn't think so," he replied. "I come to the city as little as possible."

"But we shall miss our Ellie, her ladyship, I mean," cried Elisabeth's mother.

"Oh, she can come back as often as she likes. Nothing to stop her. She can live here if she wants. Come along, Elisabeth. If you're coming with me, we must be off."

If she was going with him? Where would she go if not with her new husband? Ellie's mother and grandmother stood with their mouths open at this extraordinary pronouncement. And what did he mean, she could live in London if she wanted? Weren't they going to live together? But the Marquess simply strode off towards the carriage, with Ellie almost running to keep up with him.

Mr. Brownlow came bustling up just as the newlyweds' carriage began to move off.

"Just been talking to the Marquess's uncle," he announced loudly. "Capital fellow! Told him I could put him in the way of a good Chambertin. Seemed glad of it. Now, where's my son-in-law? Want to welcome him to the family."

"I'm afraid you just missed him, dear," said his wife, collecting her wits. "He had to get back to his estates in the country. Elisabeth has gone with him."

"Already? 'Pon my word, he's an eager one, to be sure," replied her husband with a ribald laugh. "Can't say I blame him! Eager for the wedding night and all that…"

Mrs. Brownlow blushed for her daughter's sake, but did not set him right.

James's uncle, Lord Desmond Farrell, was only too pleased to host the wedding breakfast entirely at his nephew's expense. The champagne flowed freely and the food was both costly and delicious. It had been chosen by the combined efforts of his lordship's cook and housekeeper who had served the late Marquess and knew how to maintain the standards of the House of Hastings. Toasts were drunk in their absence to the happy couple, and James's best man surprised the company by delivering a speech in which he spoke of what a good friend the Marquess was, and how often he had delivered his chums from scrapes. Mr. Brownlow was in his element, his voice too loud, eating too much and drinking too much of the champagne, all the while saying that whatever they had paid for it, he could have had it for less. His wife was held to be a charming, ladylike creature. They wondered how she put up with him.

Chapter Eighteen

Elisabeth Farrell, the new Marchioness of Hastings, sank back against the squabs of the carriage with a sigh. She had climbed in next to Nanny and spent the first few minutes calming the old lady's apologies for taking up so much space, being such a nuisance and regretting that his lordship hadn't made her travel on the stage.

Finally, James had taken his old nanny's hand, looked into her eyes and said, "If you were to travel on the stage, I would worry about you from beginning to end. You are doing me a service by agreeing to come with us like this." He then smiled his sweet smile and it was easy to see why the old lady was as devoted to him as he was to her.

"Very well, but I shall not bore you with my chatter," she said, and proceeded to tell Ellie all about her new husband when he was a boy, how clever he was, how kind, to be sure a little difficult at times, and in trouble with his Papa, but Nanny had always been able to manage him and cheer him up.

Ellie was fascinated by this glimpse into James's past. It was plain to see he had not had an easy childhood. She looked at him now, staring unseeingly out the carriage windows as they rolled through the streets of London and then into the country. He was no doubt thinking of his plans for Maylands. In his distant gaze she thought she could see the little boy, so often misunderstood and unhappy.

Nanny finally talked herself to a standstill and her head began to drop onto her chest. It wasn't surprising. Ellie had never ridden in such a well-sprung carriage, and after her own restless night she was lulled by its gentle swaying. After a while she, too, slept, and only awoke when the carriage clattered into the courtyard of a posting house and the swaying stopped.

"We'll have a luncheon here," announced his lordship. "I bespoke it and a private room, so they know we're coming. But I don't want to stop for long."

He leaped down from the carriage and started off, then appeared to bethink himself. He came back and handed Ellie down, saying, "Nanny, wait here. I'll accompany Elisabeth in and come back for you."

Nanny was still half asleep and glad of the time to arrange herself. She muttered something incoherent and nodded. James took his wife inside, where they were met by the innkeeper. He immediately took in the details of Ellie's wedding gown and drew the correct conclusion.

"Allow me to congratulate you on your marriage, my lord, my lady," he said, bowing so that his nose almost touched his knee, "and also let me say how distressed we all were to hear of your father's death. He was a fine man." He echoed the words of the butler at Maylands, meanwhile thinking exactly as he had, that the previous Marquess had always been a man to go hard at a gate, in more ways than one. He was looking forward to serving the son, who had always been much more reasonable over trifles such as a burned roast or under-cooked potatoes. He did have an odd way of staring at you, but he had never ordered a whole meal back to the kitchen and demanded another. And here he was with a pretty wife. Well, good luck to him.

"Thank you, Binns," replied his lordship. "My wife and Nanny would like the use of the chamber I bespoke. Then you may serve luncheon."

If he thought it odd for a man to invite his old Nanny on his wedding trip, Mr. Binns wisely kept his own council.

"Of course, my lord," he said, bowing again. "We have reserved the best upstairs chamber for her ladyship. I'll have the maid take her up."

"No, that will not do for Nanny, She cannot manage the stairs. We shall need something downstairs for her."

James turned to fetch his old protector, not waiting to hear the innkeeper's exclamation of dismay.

"But we've nothing free downstairs! I naturally thought, for her ladyship, the best chamber..."

But then he bethought himself, and urged a hesitating Elisabeth upstairs with the maid. Without a moment's hesitation, he went to roust a young man out of the only downstairs chamber where he lay, attempting to shake off the effects of heavy drinking most of the night before. He had apparently lost his all on a horse and had tried to drown his sorrows. The innkeeper showed him no mercy, however. He threw open the casement window to air the room, and bundled the man and his belongings out of the room into the back yard before he had a chance to protest.

"The fresh air'll do you good," he told the fellow, whose eyes had closed in anguish against the bright sunlight. "I'll bring you a glass of porter and a beef sandwich in a moment. That'll put you to rights."

The young man's stomach roiled at the idea of a beef sandwich, but the porter sounded promising, so he slumped down on a bench and nodded assent.

Calling for hot water for both the best front bedchamber and the small downstairs one, the innkeeper hastily straightened the room and pulled the bedclothes up just in time for Nanny's arrival.

"Hot water will be here directly, Madam," he said, and bowed himself out.

Meanwhile, before the maid left for the promised hot water, Ellie asked her to unhook her train on her shoulders, and then removed the wreath of roses from her head. As a result, when she went downstairs about ten minutes later, she looked a little overdressed for lunch at a country inn, but by no means as conspicuous as a bride.

Mrs. Binns was a fine cook, but sadly addicted to the bottle. As the day went on, her attention to it became greater than her attention to the food. The result was the burned roast and practically raw potatoes the late Marquess had ordered removed from his sight and replaced with something a man could eat, dammit! But today she was still almost sober. The lunch was good, though simple: a rabbit pie with a side dish of smothered leeks, a leg of lamb dressed with morels and roasted turnips, chicken livers fried with bacon and a lemon pudding to top it off.

All three ate with appetite, James because he had been preoccupied with Ellie's possible lateness at the chapel and had forgotten to eat his breakfast, Ellie because she had been too nervous about the day ahead to swallow more than a small corner of bread and butter and a mouthful of tea, and Nanny because she was particularly fond of chicken livers with bacon. Between them they finished the lemon pudding, to the disappointment of the landlord, who had been looking forward to some of it with his tea.

Chapter Nineteen

It was a comfortably full and satisfied group that climbed back into the carriage for the second half of the journey to Maylands. Ellie beguiled the journey by telling the other two what she had discovered about de Bougainville's journey to Tahiti, and wishing she had thought to take her little book out of her trunk so she could show it to them.

"He describes the island as a paradise," she said. "The fruit simply falls off the trees and the fish leap out of the water and into the nets. Crime appears to have been almost unknown until the arrival of the white men. But that may be because no one seems to have owned anything, really. Everything was held in common and what one needed, one took, or used. I wonder whether such a system could work here."

"I'd like to think so," said Nanny, "but I fear we all want to own our own things and wouldn't take kindly to someone else using them without a by-your-leave."

"I remember the beating I got for taking cousin Eustace's fishing rod that time when I was a boy," said James. "It seemed reasonable to me. He wasn't using it and I wanted to go fishing. He only made a fuss when he saw me with it."

"Yes, but don't you remember, my lord," said Nanny, "when he took it from you, you got so angry you seized it and broke it into four pieces. That's why you were beaten, not for taking it."

James's face split into a grin. "Yes I did, and by God, I'd do it again! Just to see his face when I handed him the bits. It was worth the beating! That was the same face he had when he knew I was to be married and he wouldn't get his hands on any part of Maylands!

But why should he have it? He doesn't love it as I do, just as he didn't love the fishing rod until he knew I had it. It was worth getting married for that."

He didn't seem to realize that this remark was very rude to Ellie. Her hackles rose and her immediate reaction was to say she would see whether getting away from her stepfather was worth marrying him, but she held her tongue. It was Nanny who remonstrated with him.

"Now, my lord," she said gently, "that's not a very kind thing to say to her ladyship!"

James fixed Ellie with his black stare, but after a moment he gave a wry smile. "No, I suppose it isn't," he said. "I'm sorry, Elisabeth. I didn't mean it like that. I'm glad I married you. You are much better than all those other witches."

Ellie had to laugh. "That would have been handsomely said," she said, smiling broadly, "if it hadn't been for that bit about the other *witches*. It isn't much to be preferred above a parcel of undesirables!"

"But you *are* so much better than them," he insisted. "It's nothing but the truth."

"But you still gave the impression you had rather not be married at all."

"No more would I!" he replied at once. "I didn't *want* a wife!"

"Worse and worse!" Ellie laughed again. "That's not what a new bride wants to hear! Sometimes a little lie is better than the absolute truth. You must see that. It would have been kinder to say *I'm glad I married you, Ellie. You are the perfect wife for me.*"

James thought this over for a while. "You talked about white lies before. Would you really rather I told something that wasn't absolutely true?"

It was Ellie's turn to think. How often did one tell less than the absolute truth? Quite often, it must be said. If a friend asked an opinion of a gown, or a new coiffure, did one always say what one really felt? When Mama had asked her opinion of Mr. Brownlow, Ellie had said she thought him a fine man. It wasn't true, but she hadn't wanted to hurt her feelings. That must be it: if one wished to protect the other, one might not always tell the absolute truth.

"In most things," she said slowly, "I would rather hear the unvarnished truth. But if it was something you thought would really hurt my feelings, perhaps I would prefer a white lie."

"Did I really hurt your feelings with what I said just now?"

"No, because I knew how you felt. Actually, I was a bit annoyed at first, but then I thought it was quite funny."

"So why did you tell me I should have lied?"

"Oh, James, I don't know! I just thought you *might*, to save my feelings, that's all!"

"But if you thought it was funny, I didn't need to save your feelings!"

Ellie smiled at her husband. "I can see this discussion is going round and round. The trouble with you, James, is you're too *literal*. You don't invent anything."

He looked at her with great seriousness. "I don't think I know how to invent—stories, at least. When I was a child I never liked those tales where animals speak, did I Nanny?"

"No, my lord, you didn't. You always complained it wasn't real."

"I'm afraid I'm just the opposite," said Ellie. "I invent all the time. My story about de Bougainville is half invention. And I thought I might write stories for city children to read about life in the country. The animals can tell us about themselves."

"In that case, you can write about my Princess of Maylands. That's the heifer I'm raising according to my new feeding ideas. But if she talks to the children all she'll have to say is that every day she eats delicious fodder and gets fatter. It won't be very interesting."

"Oh, I'll describe the butterflies that land on her nose, the sunlight shining through the leaves of the trees, the little creatures she sees hopping in the grass. She'll have conversations with them."

"Even though I wasn't keen on that type of thing when I was a child, I'd like to hear a conversation between my fat young heifer and a grasshopper."

"Then you shall. You can introduce me to her. I'll see what she has to say."

James looked a little puzzled then gave her his charming smile. "I *am* glad we are married," he said finally. "I like you Elisabeth. And that is not a white lie."

"And I like you, James," she responded. "And that isn't a white lie either."

They continued in a companionable silence, Nanny drowsing and the autumn sun glowing golden through the beeches. After a while, Ellie noticed that the men working in the fields stood and doffed their caps as the carriage went by, and when they clopped through the next village, the women came out of the cottages and bobbed a curtsey. This must be part of her husband's estate, Maylands. Her estate, now, she supposed.

The carriage turned into a lane that Ellie soon realized was the beginning of the driveway to Farrell Court. It wound through majestic trees until the vista suddenly cleared, and a lovely old house could be seen, standing on an eminence with a lake at the bottom. As the carriage wound around the left side of the lake and came up to the house, Ellie could see it was a three-story building of weathered grey stone with rows of tall windows at each level. The front entrance was reached by wide stone steps with an elegant pierced stone railing on either side and tall iron torchère at each end. The whole household staff was ranged on these steps as the carriage drew to a halt in front. Ellie wondered how they had known the Marquess was arriving, but realized that a fleet-footed child had probably run across the field while they were making their way up the winding drive. A footman opened the carriage door and placed a stepping stool before it. James leaped out in one bound, ignoring the stool altogether, but then stood by the door to hand out his bride. This was a marked contrast to his behavior at the inn, and Ellie smiled to herself. He had remembered her this time.

He bent inside the carriage to have a word with the old lady sitting there, and then turned to the driver. "Once the trunks are off, take Nanny home," he said. "Make sure you see her through her door." The driver touched his tall hat with his whip and nodded.

Then he turned to an elderly gentleman in a black cut-away coat. "Prewitt, this is my wife, Elisabeth. Elisabeth, Prewitt is our butler and knows more than anyone. You can ask him anything."

"My lady," intoned the butler with a bow, "Welcome to Farrell Court. We hope you will be very happy here."

He proceeded to walk at her side up the stairs, introducing the cook and the housekeeper, Mrs. Simmins. She was an older lady, somewhat stout, but erect in her carriage and very neatly dressed. As she curtseyed, she cast an expert eye over her new mistress's gown and Ellie saw a light of approval in her eye. *Thank goodness, one examination down*, she thought. The rest of the staff curtseyed or bowed and Ellie smiled at them all.

"I shall learn all your names soon, I hope," she said in a clear voice, "but I shall need you to help me!"

And she continued up the steps, through the wide-flung double doors and into her new home.

Chapter Twenty

James disappeared the minute they entered the wide hall. But Ellie had no time to wonder where he had gone, for the housekeeper was at her elbow, saying, "I've ordered tea in your apartment, your ladyship. You are no doubt tired from the trip and will want to rest before dinner. We keep early hours here at Farrell Court, so dinner is at six, unless you wish me to delay it?"

"No, by no means. Mrs. Simmins," replied Ellie. "Don't change anything on my account. Does Jam… his lordship know what time dinner is?"

The housekeeper looked at her with understanding. "We toll the chapel bell at five every evening. His lordship's nanny persuaded his father to institute the custom when he was a boy, as he was often in trouble for being late to table. Now everyone on the estate knows what time it is when the bell tolls. His late lordship often remarked how useful it was and said he was glad he had thought of it." The housekeeper gave a conspiratorial smile, which Ellie fully appreciated.

"Nanny seems to have had a very beneficial influence when he was young. No wonder he is so fond of her."

"Yes, my lady. His mother died when he was not much more than an infant, and Nanny more or less took her place. His late lordship was…," the housekeeper hesitated, "…was a good man but not… very *accommodating*, if you understand me. Nanny was very protective of the young master." She mused for a moment. "We are all very fond of him below stairs. He has spent more time down with us than anywhere else."

She said no more, but Ellie was forming a clear picture of her husband's childhood. When he was unhappy upstairs, he escaped downstairs.

"I'm glad the bell system works so well," she said, bringing the conversation back to where it started. "I'm sure cook doesn't want everything to spoil."

"Indeed not, my lady. Today she has prepared all his lordship's favorite dishes."

They had been ascending the wide staircase and now Mrs. Simmins led Ellie into a pair of fine rooms on the front of the building, obviously kept for the lady of the house. They were standing in a pleasant, light-filled sitting room from where they could see into the bedchamber. The furnishings and hangings in both were faded and old-fashioned. Ellie didn't know it, but they were in the style made popular by the designs of George Hepplewhite. The chairs and settee had shield-shaped backs and slim straight square legs tapering down to a sort of squared-off club. They were upholstered in a silk that may once have been dark red, but was now faded to a greyish pink. The graceful four-poster bed and windows were hung with the same silk, and the curtains were tied back with large corded tassels in dull gold. Despite their faded state, or perhaps because of it, the rooms were pretty and feminine without being overly frivolous.

"The rooms haven't been used since her late ladyship's time," said the housekeeper apologetically. "The furnishings and hangings need refurbishment, I'm afraid. The late Marquess never came in here after his wife's death and the present one, well, his mind is fixed on other things."

"I think it's lovely!" said Ellie, who had never had such spacious or grand accommodations in her life. "I am happy to leave it exactly as it is." Then she hesitated and added, "Does his lordship sleep next door?" She could see there was a communicating door in the bedchamber.

"No, my lady. Lord James, I'm sorry, his lordship, sleeps in the room he has used since he was a boy. It's at the other end of the wing. I can show you now, if you choose, but I thought we would do a tour of the whole house tomorrow."

"Oh, no, I mean yes," said Ellie in some confusion. "Tomorrow would be best. I... er, I'd like to settle in here first."

At that moment a pair of footmen arrived with Ellie's trunk.

"You have no dresser as yet, my lady, so I shall see to the unpacking of your things," said Mrs. Simmins.

Silently thanking her mother for her insistence on good underwear and nightgowns, Ellie replied with a nonchalance she was far from feeling, "You will find I have packed rather little. I am not accustomed to living in the country and found most of my town wear unsuitable. My modiste will be sending me some things very soon."

She hoped this was, in fact the case. She had left the chapel without seeing Mr. Sanderson, so at present she hadn't a penny to pay the dressmaker.

Both the sitting room and the bedchamber had tall windows overlooking the front of the house and the lake. Ellie went to them and looked out. From this vantage point beyond the trees that surrounded the house and grounds now striped with gold in the autumn sun, she could see the fields of the estate. There was a hay wain in one of them and she could see men tossing hay up to a tall individual in a white shirt standing on the top. They worked in a synchronized rhythm that was beautiful to behold. The village they had passed through was just visible, with the church spire in the center. It was a lovely and tranquil scene; she could see why James was so attached to it.

Thinking of her husband made her wonder where he had gone, and if he would come to see her. She was disturbed in her contemplation by a maid arriving with a tea tray. This young person bobbed a curtsey and said, "Cook's compliments, m'lady. She has sent you some macaroons, being as they're his lordship's favorite and she thought you might like some afore he gets in the kitchen and eats the lot—oh, I wasn't s'posed to say that!" She covered her mouth with her hand and her eyes were round above it.

Ellie smiled. "Oh, I already know he's a frequent visitor below stairs."

"Yes, m'lady. He's there all the time."

The maid bobbed another curtsey and left. Ellie poured herself a cup of tea and nibbled a macaroon. It was delicious. She forced herself to relax. Everyone was very pleasant. Her rooms were lovely. Even if her husband wanted... well, *that* , it couldn't be so bad, could it? Sitting there, with the late summer sun angling into the room and the distant sounds of voices on the air, she suddenly felt bone tired. The months of worry about what she should do, then the extraordinary advertisement in the newspaper, the meetings with James and Mr. Sanderson, and finally the wedding to a man she barely knew. It had all been exhausting. She rose and went into the bedroom, where Mrs. Simmins was closing the lid of the trunk, the contents evidently neatly disposed somewhere.

"I think I shall lie down for a minute," she said. "I do feel very tired." She kicked off her slippers and reached behind her back, trying to undo the tiny buttons of her wedding gown.

"Let me help you, my lady," said Mrs. Simmins, and swiftly undid them all.

Ellie stepped out of her gown and all but fell onto the wide bed. The housekeeper had pulled back the silk counterpane and the cool white sheets met her weary body. Muttering a thank you to Mrs. Simmins, she was asleep almost before her head touched the pillow. The housekeeper hung up the silk gown, drew the grey-pink curtains to shade her new mistress from the golden light, collected the tea tray and quietly left the room.

Chapter Twenty-One

By half past five Ellie was descending the stairs, having been startled awake by the sound of the five o'clock bell. She hadn't known where she was for a minute, then she wondered if her husband had been in to look for her. Perhaps she shouldn't have allowed herself to fall asleep. She found her clothing neatly put away by Mrs. Simmins and quickly dressed in one of her evening gowns, though it felt odd, for it was still full daylight outside.

She reached the bottom of the stairs and looked around. Where was the dining room? In any case, it must still be too early, for the house was very quiet. She was crossing the hall to a door that looked as if it might open to the drawing room when suddenly James erupted from the back of the house. He was coatless and his shirt was wide open at the neck, revealing glimpses of smooth black hair. He was in stockinged feet and pieces of hay were sticking from his hair and britches. He looked so very masculine that something inside Ellie gave a lurch. She felt suddenly breathless, and was both relieved and a little put out when she realized he obviously wasn't thinking about her at all. He was munching on something and when he lifted his hand to his mouth, she saw it was a macaroon. He stopped short when he saw her.

"Oh!" he said swallowing, " Er... Elisabeth! I... um..."

"James!" said Ellie and added rather stupidly, "I thought you might have been looking for me, but I see you've been in the fields."

His mouth split in a wide grin. "Yes, I've been helping with the haymaking. Fine fun it was too. Why did you think I'd been looking for you?"

She didn't know how to answer. Suddenly she remembered what she had seen from her windows. "Was that you on the top of the hay wain?"

"Yes! They tried to stop me, but Jessemy had just fallen off and was winded. I took his place."

In spite of her confusion, she was intrigued. "Isn't it dangerous?"

"Only if you fall on a pitchfork!" he gave his characteristic bark of laughter. "But I don't fall. Never have. I didn't mean to start in with it, but, well, once I saw they needed me…"

And you didn't think I might need your help, I suppose, said Ellie to herself. *All alone in a strange house on my wedding day*. But aloud she said, "I don't know where you found the energy. After the last few days I was exhausted. I fell asleep as soon as I saw my bed, I'm afraid."

Then she blushed. The word *bed* suddenly struck her as so loaded.

But it was lost on her husband. "I love to work!" he said, "Especially when I see how much more productive the estate is now. The men tell me we've harvested more than twice the clover hay this year."

Luckily for Ellie, who was trying to reconcile her sensitivity with her husband's oblivion, they were interrupted by the butler, who came into the hall bearing a tray with a bottle and glasses. "My lord!" he said, when he saw the Marquess. "I was bringing in the sherry, but…"

"I'm on my way to get changed. Send Furber up, would you? But perhaps Elisabeth, er… her ladyship, would like some sherry," said James. He gave her his charming smile and her heart lurched again. "Sorry to keep you waiting."

"I don't mind waiting," she replied, "and I do enjoy a sherry, if it isn't too dry."

"It probably is. My father bought the stuff that's so dry your tongue sticks to the roof of your mouth," said James. "Is that what you've got there, Prewitt?"

"Er, yes, sir, I'm afraid it is."

"Well please go and find something else. Neither of us likes it."

"Perhaps some champagne, my lord? To celebrate your wedding?"

"Good idea, Prewitt!" James beamed. "You always know best! They said I couldn't find and marry a wife in four months, and I did. And a very nice one." He smiled at her again. "I won't be long."

He leaped up the stairs, two at a time. The butler bowed and went away with the tray.

Ellie was in utter confusion. What was the matter with her? She had reconciled herself to a marriage of convenience and had been dreading anything else. But James was handsome, charming and… and well, desirable. She wished she knew what he was thinking. He was obviously glad she was his wife, but did he still only think of her as a solution to his inheritance problems? Would he want her to be more than that? What was he planning for… for later on? Should she ask him? *Could* she ask him? What on earth would she say? *Oh, by the way, James, are you planning on consummating the marriage tonight, whatever that means. And if you are, I don't mind?* She shook her head. No, definitely not.

Shaking her head as if to rid it of these disturbing thoughts, she continued crossing the wide hall into the large drawing room. It must be right under her bedroom, she judged, for it had a similar view, over the lake, at a lower angle. The furnishings down here were similar to those upstairs, though instead of pink the upholstery was in a color between yellow and beige, also much faded. It was a pleasant, welcoming room. Ellie thought of the former Lady Hastings who had no doubt been responsible for its furnishings. Would she ever feel entitled to think of it as her own, to change if she wished?

Prewitt came back with a bottle of champagne, two glasses and a plate of little pink biscuits.

"His lordship may be a moment, my lady," he said. "Shall I open the bottle now?"

Ellie was going to say no, but then thought again. If, as she believed, her husband was still only thinking of her as a solution to his inheritance problems, why shouldn't she drink on her own?

"Yes, please, Prewitt," she said. "I can't imagine his lordship will object."

"No, indeed," responded the butler seriously. "I hope you won't mind my saying it, my lady, he has his funny ways, but he is a good, kind man. You won't find a soul in these parts who says different."

He poured her a glass and waited for her to taste it, before wrapping it back in its linen napkin. Then he said, with a little hesitation, "May I say, my lady, that the staff would like the occasion to drink to your and his lordship's health. It's not the sort of thing he is likely to think of. Perhaps you could mention it to him? After dinner?"

Just as Ellie was about to agree to this suggestion, James strode into the room, his hair still wet from obviously rushed ablutions, but otherwise looking well turned out. He really was very handsome.

"Who isn't likely to think of what? Me, I suppose!" he said, grinning.

Ellie couldn't help smiling. "Prewitt was just suggesting that the staff would like to drink our health after dinner."

"He's right! I told you, Elisabeth, butlers are always right. I wouldn't have thought of it, but it's a good idea. Just give us the word, Prewitt and we'll bowl on down to the kitchen. Besides, that way I can see if there are any macaroons left." His eye fell on the tray Prewitt had brought in. "Oh good, pink biscuits. I like those too. Eating pink biscuits with champagne was just about the only thing I learned when I went to Paris with my father that time. Well, perhaps not quite the only thing." He smiled at a secret thought. He picked up a biscuit and gobbled it down.

Ellie laughed. "You appear to have a sweet tooth, my lord. Or are you just very hungry?"

"I'm always hungry! Talking of which, drink up, Elisabeth! Dinner must be on the table. It's gone six." He grabbed the glass of champagne Prewitt had poured for him and raised his glass to her, before swallowing in great gulps.

"I'll inform cook that you're ready, my lord," said the butler and glided out.

"Surely it won't be on the table if you're not there?" Ellie was puzzled.

James thought for a moment. "No, I suppose you're right. I keep forgetting my father isn't here. He was very particular about dinner being on the table at six. I can't tell you how many times I was sent away without eating when I was a boy because I arrived late."

"Perhaps that's why you're always hungry now."

"Oh no! All I had to do was go down to cook and she fed me. Couldn't let father know, of course. But he never went into the kitchens, whereas I was nearly always there."

All the people below stairs seemed to have loved and protected him, she reflected. Nanny, the housekeeper, the butler and now the cook. For Ellie, who had grown up with two very loving parents, it seemed strange.

James led her down the hall into an enormous dining room. It was very grand, its ochre-colored walls covered with dark oil paintings featuring animals and birds in various stages of death, and with a huge dining table down the center. Ellie counted thirty chairs, with more ranged along the walls.

"Gracious!" she said, "surely we aren't going to sit at each end of this?"

From where they stood, they could see two places set, one close to them and the other at the far end of the gleaming mahogany surface. Several branched candelabra stood along its length, and in the middle was a huge silver object that appeared to be four nymphs in flowing robes holding up a dish, from the center of which rose columns supporting a second dish. The lower was filled with apples, pears, plums and grapes, and the top with nuts of various sorts.

"My father liked eating in here with the table set like this and we've never thought to change it. When I was here on my own I ate in the kitchen most of the time. But I agree," James laughed, "I won't be able to see you over that lot! Let's go into the breakfast room. Come on."

He pulled her out the door and down to a much smaller room on the other side of the hall. Its table seated a mere twelve and it was more cheerful, with a large vase of gladioli in the center.

"I'll just go and tell Prewitt we're in here. Someone will come and set the covers."

"I could go and get them from the dining room," suggested Ellie.

"Better not. I think that's the dining room silver. We've got another set for in here. At least, I got in trouble once for mixing it all up. I was playing armies with the knives and forks."

"You seem to have been in trouble a lot when you were younger," remarked Ellie.

"Yes. I suppose I was."

With that, he left her and Ellie could hear him thudding down the back stairs, shouting, "Prewitt! We're dining in the breakfast room."

In due course a footman and maid came in to remove the gladioli and lay the table with, presumably, the correct silver. James came back, munching what proved to be another macaroon, then dinner arrived, and they sat down, nearly an hour late.

"Good thing your Papa isn't here," said Ellie, and then realized what she had said. "I mean, because we're so late. Not because he… well…"

James gave his bark of laughter. "He'd ring a fine peal over us both, that's certain! But he'd be glad I'm married, so perhaps he would forgive us."

"Why was he so determined you should find a wife?"

"For an heir, of course. My cousin is next in line after me, and he has only a daughter. Unless there's a boy, the name will die out."

"Oh, I see."

Now was the time for Ellie to ask her difficult question. Was he or wasn't he going to visit her later? But looking at him tucking into his beef apparently without a care in the world, she simply could not. She applied herself to her own meal. The cook had obviously taken great care and the dishes were delicious and varied, but it was hard to enjoy them, as disturbed as she was.

After dinner they went down to the kitchen to receive the toast from the staff. Prewitt made a nice little speech, wished them both very happy, and the champagne was drunk. Ellie just had time for a brief word of thanks to cook for the delicious dinner, when James made signs he was ready to leave. He was carrying the boots and coat he'd obviously worn before, as they still had hay stuck to them. On the way out he spoke to the man Ellie recognized as the head groom.

It was still before nine o'clock when they were back in the hall. The sun had set but it was not yet fully dark.

"I'm going to visit my young heifer," said James. "I just told Truman to bring my horse round. I was going to see her before, but got involved in the hay-making. You'll probably be asleep by the time I get back, so I'll see you tomorrow. Goodnight!"

He went cheerfully out the front door and a few minutes later, Ellie heard the sound of a horse on the gravel. He was gone.

Well, said Ellie to herself. *It seems I've been making a May game of myself wondering about my wedding night. Whatever made me think I might be the female my husband is interested in? My fears have been for naught!* She laughed softly, not knowing if she was glad or disappointed. Then she shrugged her shoulders and went upstairs for a shawl. She would take a walk.

Chapter Twenty-Two

There was no one in the hall when Ellie came downstairs. She ran lightly across the wide area between the stairs and the big double doors, opened one and slipped outside. It was a lovely, calm evening, warm and still quite light from the sun just below the horizon. The air was perfumed with what she recognized as phlox. The scent came from a heavily planted flower bed beyond the gravel path in front of the wide steps up to the house. It immediately took her back to a walk with her father around their rather ramshackle estate when she was a child.

"How can a man be poor," he had said, "when he has this perfume at his door?"

She hadn't been back to the old place since her father died. Her uncle had not seemed to want to keep the family ties together, or perhaps he was afraid that if he invited Ellie and her mother, they might expect more in the way of maintenance. But the perfume of the flowers brought it all back, and she felt a sadness well up in her heart.

Mentally, she gave herself a shake. It was unlike her to indulge in a fit of the dismals, and she told herself to buck up. She walked along the flower bed until she came to the end of the house, then turned and walked around the side of the house. She passed an open door with a flickering light in the depths below, and a different scent, this time of roasted meat, came to her nose. That must be the back door to the kitchen, much used by her husband. Off to her right she could see the outline of glass houses and the shape of a hedge against the sky. The kitchen gardens, probably.

She turned the corner to the back of the house and the smell of horses told her she was nearing the stables. As she came closer, she could see the wide doors were open and three men were sitting on upturned barrels playing cards by the light of lanterns hung from beams outside the stalls. Some of the horses had their heads over the half-doors of their stalls and were watching the men, for all the world as if they were interested in the play. Her spirits lifted and she thought what a nice picture that would make for her children's book about life in the country.

She didn't want to disturb the men or the horses, and stayed in the shadows as she walked by, around the other side of the house and back to the front. The moon was not visible and it was by now almost fully dark. She smelled the phlox again and smiled as she mounted the steps to the front door.

Someone had lit a large branched candelabrum on the hall table. It threw a flickering light over the stone floor and played on the blades of a pair of crossed swords hung upon the wall. She saw now this was a physical representation of the coat of arms on the sides of her husband's carriage. Underneath the swords hung a painted motto: *Honor et Virtus.* She knew that *virtus* meant not *virtue* but *strength*. The crossed swords supported that idea. Did James come from a line of warriors? As she climbed the stairs, she imagined him in a breastplate and helmet, brandishing a sword. Yes, she decided, he would look very fine.

Candles had also been lit in her rooms, where the bed had been remade and the curtains drawn. There was still warmish water in the jug on the washstand behind the screen in the corner of her bedchamber, so she washed her hands and face and brushed her teeth. The hem of her evening gown was dusty from her walk, so she hung it up, promising to brush it in the morning. She extinguished all the candles and found her way by feel to her bed. Once again, she fell onto the cool sheets and in a few minutes was sound asleep.

Though he came in whistling, she did not hear her husband return an hour or so later, but how could she? His bedchamber was far from hers and he mounted the back stairs. He was well pleased with the progress his Princess was making. At nine months, she already weighed over 500 pounds and was gaining at the rate of a pound a day. By the time she bore her first calf she would be a mighty matron, and it was to be hoped the calf would follow the mother. He did not spare a thought for his wife, but like her, he fell asleep very quickly. It had been a long day.

Both were awake early the next morning, James because it was his habit, and Elisabeth because she had fallen asleep early. She was already sitting up in bed when the maid crept in with hot water.

"Oh! M'lady!" she said, bobbing a curtsey. "If I'd a-known you was awake I'd a-brought you a cup of tea."

"No matter! If cook is ready, I'll have breakfast downstairs. What time does his lordship usually go down?"

"He's an early riser, m'lady! He gen'rally takes something in the kitchen on his way out the door. But I'll tell cook you'll be down d'reckly." The maid bobbed a curtsey again and was gone before Ellie could say anything more.

Consequently, she was in the breakfast room sipping a cup of tea and contemplating a plate of warm muffins when James came striding in with a friendly greeting.

"Good morning, Elisabeth! Cook wouldn't let me gobble something at the kitchen table as I usually do. She said I was to breakfast with you. She's quite right, of course. I must remember."

Ellie was about to ask if it was her existence he must remember, but was prevented by Prewitt coming in with a huge plate of eggs, bacon and what looked like half a loaf of bread and a pound of butter.

"Hope you don't mind if I begin, but I'm hungry," said her husband, and without waiting for an answer, fell to.

It was impossible to converse with him while he was eating with such rapidity, so Ellie waited a moment. But this time, she was about to speak when Prewitt came in with coffee. He poured a cup for his lordship, and asked Ellie with a bow if she needed more tea, muffins, or anything else he might be able to furnish her with.

"A little more hot water for the tea, please, Prewitt," she smiled. "I've already drunk the pot dry. I'm so thirsty this morning."

"The champagne, I expect," said James. "Always makes me damned thirsty. I remember in Paris that time, when I woke up in the morning with a head like a bear and I went to drink the water from the washbasin jug and… er, " his voice tailed off.

"What happened?" asked Ellie, intrigued.

"Oh, nothing, really. She… I mean the… the maid said it wasn't fit to drink. She had to bring me water in bottles."

"The normal water isn't good?"

"No, apparently not."

"I wonder why."

"I don't know, but here in the country," said James, "you have to be careful not to dig too close to places with animal sh… er, waste. It gets in the water."

"Yes, I suppose it does," replied Ellie, still a little puzzled by where this whole conversation began. But then Prewitt came back with more hot water for the teapot and the moment passed.

"What are you doing today?" she asked her husband, who had finished his meal and showed every sign of getting ready to leave the table. "Mrs. Simmins is showing me over the house this morning, but I was hoping you might take me around the estate this afternoon."

"Sorry, Elisabeth. Too busy. Anyway, you couldn't possibly see it all in an afternoon. But if you want to ride around, just tell the stables to saddle you up a horse."

"But I don't ride!"

"Don't ride?" James was astonished. "Whyever not?"

"I never learned, I'm a city girl, you know."

Her husband stared at her in amazement. Then he said, "Well, tell Truman to get the gig ready. Can you manage a gig?"

"I can, but I'm nervous when I don't know where I'm going. I'd like someone who knows the estate to drive me around at first."

She was hoping he would volunteer. But no.

"Hmm," he said, thinking. "I'm seeing Fletcher this morning. He's the estate manager. I'll arrange to have him take you over the whole place. It won't be today, though, I need him. But if you want to just go out for a bit, have Prewitt send someone to the stables for the gig and a groom. I doubt I'll be in for luncheon, but I'll see you at dinner. Goodbye!"

And with that, on the first morning of his married life, the bridegroom was gone, leaving his wife staring into her teacup at the breakfast table.

Chapter Twenty Three

After breakfast, Elisabeth went upstairs to brush the hem of her evening dress, but found it gone. Her bed was remade and in perfect order. She realized she must get used to doing nothing for herself. She was looking out of the windows over the lake which lay covered in an early morning mist, when Mrs. Simmins came in, and the tour of the house began.

With her chatelaine of keys at her waist, Mrs. Simmins took her new mistress into every part of Farrell Court, from the attics to the cellars.

"I don't expect you will have need to come up here again," she said as they climbed the grand flights of stairs rising from the hall, to access the simpler wooden stairs to the attics. "But you will want to know what is in here. And the servants' quarters are up here at the other end."

In fact, the attics intrigued Elisabeth. She was fascinated by the remnants of bygone eras that lay, or hung, or were concealed in boxes in that dim and dusty treasure trove. Hanging from the rafters were the wide hoops that ladies wore beneath their skirts twenty years before. They were fashioned from circular strips of willow or whalebone, held in concentric circles by ribbons of fabric, now discolored and brittle.

"They are too wide to put in any of the trunks," explained the housekeeper, "Her late ladyship used them, of course, and I suppose we have not wanted to get rid of them."

"I've read that ladies liked them because it freed their legs of hampering petticoats," remarked Ellie, "but how they managed to get through doors, or into carriages, I don't know."

"It's true that we ladies often sacrifice a good deal for fashion," answered Mrs. Simmins, "though the present style for slim gowns is a much easier one to adopt. If one has the shape, which some of us do not!"

Since the housekeeper herself was a rather stout lady of more than middle years, Ellie could find nothing to say to that.

She poked around the boxes and found a trove of yellowed baby clothes. She held a couple of them up: an infant gown with a heavy lace edge, a heavy cotton long-sleeved dress with a round collar, a knitted jacket, now stiff and grey.

"Were these his lordship's?" she asked, amused to imagine her tall husband in those tiny things.

"Yes, my lady. I'm surprised those things are still there. I thought we'd given it all to the parish after her ladyship died."

"It's hard to imagine his lordship as a baby. What was he like?"

"Oh, he was so serious! He would look at things as if he was trying to work out what they were: shadows on the wall, the candles, the curtains waving in the wind. He would lie there, staring at them for hours. The sunshine making rainbows on the crystal chandeliers used to make him smile. And what a lovely smile he had, dear little mite." The old housekeeper was lost in her reminiscences for a moment, then went on. "When he was old enough to crawl and wanted to reach something, if you stopped him, my, how he cried! There was nothing for it but to let him have it. Otherwise he would scream himself into a lather. But once he was a bit older, you could explain things to him and most times he would listen. Nanny knew how to handle him. And quick! He learned things in a trice! He could do up his own buttons and tie his laces when he was not much more than a baby. 'I'm a big boy' he would say, when he was still just a wee mite! There's a painting of him with his Mama in the long gallery. I'll show you when we go down there."

Ellie reflected that the baby had become the man: the same intensity, the same single-mindedness, the same sweet smile.

They then visited the servants' quarters at the other end of the floor. These were small, cell-like rooms each with two metal framed beds, the women and men's accommodations separated by a stout door. They were actually at roof level, and light came in through small dormer windows from which one could see the tiles of the roof and the chimneys. Beneath them were the family and guest room wings. The guest rooms, graciously sized and most in pairs with communicating doors, had obviously not been used in years. The furniture was swathed in holland covers and the curtains drawn.

"It's many years since we've had house parties, my lady," said Mrs. Simmins, a little wistfully. "I remember, though, when all these rooms were filled, and we seated as many as thirty for dinner every night. But after her ladyship died, the late Marquess spent most of his time in London. He only came for the hunting and shooting. He died at the last hunt of the season in April, as I'm sure you know."

Ellie did not know, and the housekeeper told her the sorry tale. They were by now walking towards the family wing. They saw James's room. It held a narrow bed and tall bookshelves covered the walls. As well as books, these contained all sorts of items typical of boyhood, from wooden sail boats, a football and a cricket bat, to found objects such as odd-shaped stones and twigs, a large wasps' nest and a tiny birds' one. There was a desk next to the bed, laden with books and pieces of paper written all over with calculations and indecipherable formulae.

The nursery was close by. Its contents were also disguised beneath holland covers, but Ellie told herself she would come back and look for the children's books she was sure were under there, somewhere. Finally, they peeped into the room adjoining hers. This had obviously been the late Marquess's room for though it was scrupulously clean and empty, it was still redolent of tobacco or snuff. Ellie sniffed appreciatively.

"I'm afraid *nothing* will remove that smell, my lady. The late Marquess enjoyed snuff and the scent on his clothing permeated the cupboards. I don't know what to do about it."

"I quite like it," said Ellie, "and if no one else is using the room, it really doesn't matter, does it?"

The next floor down held a long ballroom at one end and a gallery in the other. The two rooms together took up the full length of the house. Both rooms were dark and shrouded, but Mrs. Simmins threw open the curtains to the windows all along one side of the gallery, the better to see the family portraits that lined the opposite wall.

"The present Marquess is the sixth in the line," explained the housekeeper, "and portraits of all his forebears are hanging here. And the ladies of the house have always used this gallery for their promenades when the weather was inclement. His lordship used to like to strap skates to his boots and sail up and down. You can see the parquet is dented from it. The late Marquess wasn't any too pleased when he found out, and he put a stop to it."

Ellie started at one end and slowly walked to the other. It was an education in the costume of ladies and gentlemen over the previous two hundred years. For the ladies, there were skirts of greater or lesser width, from the Elizabethan period when they were held wide almost parallel to the waist, with ruffed bodices, tightly laced and pointed, to those in the style of the French Court, less than fifty years ago, supported by hoops like those in the attics, the bodice cut low enough to expose nearly all the bosom. For the gentlemen, it was the width of the pantaloons that varied: from skin-tight hose topped by a puffy doublet, to more generously cut garments with coats of varied length and gorgeous design. There were high boots, low boots, shoes with square toes, shoes with pointed toes, shoes with buckles and shoes without. The women were often surrounded by their children, clothed in dresses that, unlike the adult garments, changed remarkably little over the years. The gentlemen were more often accompanied by dogs or horses, fine beasts who were intended, no doubt, to convey the superiority of their owner, much as the children in the other portraits were intended to show the fecundity of the women chosen as their wives.

It was in the third Marquess that Ellie finally found a resemblance to her husband. He had the same black hair as James and his dark eyes stared straight out of the portrait. Her husband's father and grandfather were handsome men, but it was his great-grandfather who gave him his characteristic look. At the far end she saw the portrait of James with his mother. He was an infant in a long white gown with deep lace—perhaps the very one she had seen in the attic—lying in the lap of a pretty fair lady with a wan smile. In the painting the baby's eyes were fixed upon a distant horizon.

"That is certainly his lordship," said Ellie. "He hasn't changed a bit."

The rest of the tour took in the ground floor rooms: those she had seen, plus the billiard room, the library, the gun room, the estate office and sundry rooms that seemed to serve no particular purpose. The basement was last. The house was built so that it was only half below ground; there were high narrow windows in all the rooms, from which the scudding clouds and blue sky could be seen. The back door she had seen the night before was up a short flight of steps. She saw the kitchen, the scullery, the laundry, the bad-weather drying and airing room, the servants' dining room, Mr. Prewitt's parlor, and to Ellie's relief, after inspecting the linen and china cupboards and refusing an invitation to inspect the wine rooms, Mrs. Simmins' comfortable room where she could sit and enjoy a cup of tea.

"Goodness!" she said at last, sinking into a chair. "What a very large house it is!"

"Yes," agreed Mrs. Simmins. "A home for a large family."

Ellie made no response. What could she say?

After luncheon, which she took in splendid isolation in the breakfast room, Ellie went up to her rooms, where she spent an hour lying on her bed and thinking about the book she would write about life in the country. But try as she would to concentrate, her thoughts strayed more and more to the image of the baby lying in the lap of his mother, staring not at her, but at some distant object only he could see.

Finally she got up and went to the standish in her sitting room where Mrs. Simmins had put her Tahiti book and her sketch pad. She sharpened her pencil and took it and the pad to the round table in the center of the room, drew up a chair and began.

In the center of the first page she wrote:

The Life Of An Odd Boy

At the top of the following pages she wrote:

As a baby, he would stare for hours at shadows and flickering lights.

He smiled at the sparkle of the sun on the chandeliers.

When he could crawl, if he couldn't reach something, he would make a fuss.

He could do up his buttons when he was very small.

And he tied his own shoes.

I'm a big boy, he said, when he wasn't.

When he was a bit bigger he was in trouble for making armies with the knives and forks.

He skated in the portrait gallery and was in trouble for marking the parquet.

And if he was late for dinner, which was often, he didn't get any.

She stopped. What else had she been told about her husband? She thought for moment and then decided she would have to ask Nanny.

For the rest of the afternoon, Ellie began making sketches under the headings. She became so absorbed that she was astonished when the chapel bell rang at five o'clock. She started up, gathered together her papers and put them in the drawer of the standish, both exhilarated at what she had begun, and ashamed that she had found inspiration in the difficult life of her husband. But even she had to admit, the pictures were adorable. Who wouldn't love such a boy?

Chapter Twenty-Four

She quickly washed her face and hands and dressed in the second of her evening gowns. By a little after half past five she was in the drawing room and a few minutes later, James came in, neatly turned out.

"Elisabeth!" he said, his face lighting with a smile. "Did you have a nice day? I did!"

"Yes, it was very interesting. Mrs. Simmins took me all over the house. I saw the portraits of your ancestors in the gallery. You look very like your great-grandfather."

"That's what my father always said. He said I acted like him too. He didn't seem to like him very much. Said he used to stare at him just like I did. I didn't know what he meant."

"You do stare at people, you know," said Ellie with a little hesitation, "but only if you're interested in what they say."

"Then I'm surprised I stared at my father. All he ever did was find fault with me. I wasn't at all interested in what he had to say." He grinned.

His grin was so engaging, Ellie had to smile. She changed the subject. "Anyway, you said you had a good day. What did you do?"

"I rode around chatting with the farmers about the crop yields, had a bite to eat in one of the cottages, then went to see the Princess. She was enjoying her luncheon in the top pasture by then, though it was indistinguishable from her breakfast and would no doubt soon be confused with her tea." He grinned again. "She didn't even lift her head. If you decide to write a book about the animals in the country, and you want her to say anything, you're going to have to try to catch her between meals. It won't be easy."

Ellie was surprised he remembered their conversation in the carriage, and was about to say she had started on a different book, when she thought he might not quite like it, so stopped herself. "Er... yes, I am getting ideas. Last night I went for a walk outside and saw the men playing cards in the stables. The horses looked very interested. I could imagine them saying 'I wouldn't play that card, if I were you!'"

James laughed. "Talking of horses, did you go out in the gig today?"

"No, I was... er, busy with some sketching after luncheon and I didn't have time."

"Well, Fletcher is coming tomorrow morning at ten to take you on a tour. You said you wanted to see the place. Oh, hello, Prewitt! What have you got for us there?"

The butler had entered silently with his tray and now set it down. "Since my lord and lady have no taste for his late lordship's dry sherry, I brought up this Madeira. Would you care to try it?" He looked from one to the other enquiringly.

"Yes please," said Ellie, and James nodded.

They sat companionably in silence sipping their drink until the butler returned to tell his lady that dinner was served. They chatted of this and that as they ate, and afterwards James announced he was off to see his Princess again.

"They weigh her every evening and I like to see how much she's put on," he said. "Goodnight, Elisabeth." Without waiting for an answer, he strode towards the kitchen stairs and the stables.

The next day, the estate manager drove her around the estate and she found herself the object of much interest as they clip-clopped through the village and around the edges of the fields. Everyone stopped what they were doing; the men doffed their caps and stood to attention. The women curtseyed. The children stared at her, mouths open, as if they had never seen such an apparition.

"There hasn't been a Lady at Maylands for a long time, my lady," explained Fletcher, "They're used to his lordship, but you are a new thing altogether!"

Ellie wondered when her new clothing would arrive from Hélène. She realized now what Mr. Sanderson had meant. She was the Lady and had to look the part. For that day she had been forced to put on her old cloak and bonnet. She saw that they had been well brushed and the bonnet even refurbished as far as it could be, but she still felt decidedly shabby.

Around one o'clock, the estate manager drew the gig into the yard of a well-kept farmhouse. As she was helped down from the gig, a round-faced woman came to the door, bobbed a curtsey and said, "My lady, do-ee just come in now and take a bite. It's mighty weary you must be, bumping around all morning on those lanes. I don't doubt you'll like a nice cup of tea."

"This is Mrs. Yeats," said the estate manager. "His lordship asked her to give you luncheon today. He says he'd rather eat one of her pies than a dinner at the finest restaurant in London."

"Oh, go on with you!" said Mrs. Yeats, pleased just the same. "Not but it's true I've been giving my pies to Master James, his lordship as he is now, since he were but a lad. A lovely boy he was and a lovely man he is, as we all know in these parts. And you're as welcome as him, my lady."

Ellie smiled and thanked her and was led into a large, stone-flagged kitchen, filled with the comforting smells of baking. A flitch of ham hung from the rafters in one corner, together with bunches of dried herbs and plaited strings of onions. An enormous black kettle was steaming on one side of the hearth. Urging Ellie to "set yourself down, do!" Mrs. Yeats picked it up as if it were a feather and poured boiling water into a pretty blue and white teapot. This she brought to the table and placed it in front of Ellie, along with matching teacups, a milk jug and a sugar bowl.

"Ay! I see you looking at my lovely tea set, my lady! "'Twas Master James himself gave me that when he'd been away to Lunnon—six year ago it was. Said it was to thank me for all my pies. As if he needed to thank me, God bless him! Do you pour yourself and Mr. Fletcher a cup, now, while I see to the pie."

Ellie did as she was bid and they both watched as Mrs. Yeats brushed the coals off the top of an enormous black iron pot sitting to one side of the fire. Armed with a heavy folded piece of linen, she removed the lid and extracted a huge beautifully browned pie, which she brought to the table and placed in front of them.

"I've just done a bit of cabbage and a few stewed apples to go with it," she announced, bringing over what looked like a trough of the one and a washbasin of the other. "And I baked you a nice little plum cake, should you like to try it, my lady." This was accompanied by the plunking down of a cake the size of a cartwheel.

Ellie looked in amazement at all the food laid before them.

"But... but, this can't be all for us, surely," she stammered, "You must be expecting other people!"

"Lord bless you, my lady! This is just a bite! My boys could eat this up while they was a-waiting for their supper! Now, let me cut you a piece of my pie!"

When Ellie protested she couldn't possibly eat the piece of pie Mrs. Yeats was proposing to serve her, her hostess grudgingly moved her knife and cut a smaller piece, declaring it wasn't enough to feed a kitten. The crust was flaky, the beef and mushroom filling tender and wonderfully savory. It truly was the best she had ever eaten. Still, by the time she had finished it, together with a serving of the vegetables less than half the size her hostess had wanted to give her, and eaten a sliver of the densely delicious plum cake, Ellie felt she might never be able to eat again. In fact, after thanking Mrs. Yeats sincerely for the wonderful meal, Ellie told Fletcher she would have to walk a few miles before being comfortable enough to ride again.

James gave his bark of laughter when he heard about it that evening. "I know," he said. "I am a good trencherman, as I'm sure you have observed, but she tells me I eat like a girl. She compares me to her sons, mountainous men, all three of them. They can eat a pie each, she says, and no wonder! You should see them work! They can harvest a field in a tenth of the time it takes anyone else. We used to have competitions amongst the farmers, chopping wood, hoeing up a row of turnips, that sort of thing, but they won every year, so the others gave up."

Ellie wondered if she would ever have a son capable of hoeing up a row of turnips, or indeed, if she would ever have a son at all.

Chapter Twenty-Five

Ellie's days quickly fell into a pattern. Her husband was so clearly eager to be gone in the mornings that she stopped going down for breakfast and took it in her room. She would occupy herself during the day, and meet her husband in the drawing room before six. They would dine together, then James would leave to see the female who occupied his thoughts.

When he was with her, Ellie found her husband good company. Her disappointment was that she didn't see enough of him. She saw him for a total of perhaps three hours a day. She knew that for many wives, this might be more than enough, but the more she was with him, the more Ellie both liked and was attracted to her husband. Her heart rose when she saw him, either striding in from a day's work as he had that first day, boots off, shirt undone, straw or twigs in his hair, or coming downstairs after being tidied up by his valet, handsome in his smooth pantaloons, well-cut coat and necktie that stayed impeccable for about an hour, until he began to pull it away from around his neck as if it choked him. He would rip it off before going out to see his Princess.

To Ellie's relief, a package arrived from Mr. Sanderson containing a hundred pounds. He apologized for not giving it to her at the wedding, as promised, but said her departure had been so precipitate that he had not had time. This money was intended for incidental purchases. If she had bills to pay she should send them to him and he would settle them. He hoped she and his lordship were doing well and wished them every happiness.

This advice came in good time, for the next day, several large boxes arrived containing the clothing Hélène had made up for her. The quite staggering bill was enclosed, but since the boxes contained two wool walking gowns with matching cloaks, gloves and bonnets, four warm day dresses and a long-sleeved evening gown with two shawls, she felt the *modiste* had done all she promised. She quickly forwarded the bill to the solicitor.

In one way the new wardrobe was a relief. At last she felt she could look the part of Marchioness. In another way it was no relief at all, for it was all still play-acting as far as she was concerned. As long as the marriage remained unconsummated, she knew in law she was no more the Marchioness than the man in the moon.

To keep her mind off these lowering thoughts, Ellie filled her days with activity. After three trips with the estate manager, she felt she knew her way around fairly well and said that so long as the stable furnished her with a very docile horse, she could manage the gig herself. At first, a groom always accompanied her, but as it became her habit to stop for long periods and sketch things that caught her eye, and she felt more discomfort having him waiting around with nothing to do than from being alone, she soon said she would go by herself.

One of the first places she visited was Nanny's cottage. It was not far away, within the grounds of Farrell Court itself. She had written a note to say she was coming, and even though it obviously cost her an effort, the old lady was standing in her doorway when she arrived. Cook had sent over a dish of the chicken livers with bacon that Nanny was so fond of, and some small jam tarts that she said could go with their tea. These were received with protests that they were over-generous, that Nanny herself had made a seed cake, and that it was too good of my lady to come to see her so soon after her arrival at Maylands and how was she settling in? Was there anything that Nanny could do to help? Her eyes were not so good these days, but she could still hem some sheets if they were needed.

After this initial flood was over, the tea had been made and the seed cake cut, and a minor fuss averted (wouldn't her ladyship prefer the jam tarts, they were bound to be so much better than Nanny's old cake), Ellie asked the questions she had come to ask. What was her husband like as a little boy?

If the previous speech had been a flood, this called for a deluge of biblical proportions. Nanny waxed eloquent on her favorite subject. Poor child, to lose his mama so young! Oh my goodness, what a wonderful boy he had been! So kind and giving! To be sure, he had a temper and would shout and rage so's you could hear him all over the house. Many's the time Nanny had to pick up things he had thrown to the ground when he was cross, but it was because people didn't understand what he wanted to do. He was just so clever, and he didn't like to be told no. The story of the broken fishing rods (which Ellie had forgotten) was re-told, and the time he had thrown a dinner plate against the wall, and oh my goodness, the whippings he had received. It had made Nanny so sad.

"But then," said the old lady finally, "I told him if he continued that way, people would always think him a child. To be an adult he needed to control himself. To close his eyes and silently count to ten before doing or saying anything. And he did. He would make fists by his side like this," and Nanny clenched her misshapen old fingers into the semblance of a fist, "and close his eyes. I knew he was counting. After that he almost never lost his temper. You could tell he was very angry, but he never let it show. And you know what I think, my lady?" the old lady held Ellie's knee in a surprisingly strong grip. "I think all his troubles helped him in the end. He grew into a fine man. The finest in the county. Ask anyone."

"Everyone I've spoken to certainly thinks so," said Ellie. "Thanks to you, Nanny. No wonder he loves you so much."

Ellie left Nanny after a second piece of cake and a third cup of tea and went home, turning it all over in her mind. She imagined pictures of a boy throwing his dinner against the wall and snapping a fishing rod. It made her want to smile and weep at the same time.

Since the weather continued fine, most days Ellie went out to sketch for her *Life In The Country* book. She drove herself, but was rarely alone for long. As she sat by the side of the road on a little stool provided by the stables, sketching butterflies, grasshoppers, woodlice, and the other minute life scurrying in the grass, working men would pass by to and from the fields and raise their caps, women on their way to gather hazelnuts or mushrooms or pull the entwined hops from the hedgerows to make homebrew would bob a curtsey, and children would stop to see what she was doing. They were the most curious, fascinated by her sketches.

One day, one of the younger children asked, "Why'sum you drewed a picture of a cheeseybob, m'lady?"

"Cheeseybob? What's that?" she answered.

"Dem's cheeseybobs," said the child, indicating the woodlice she had just drawn.

These little creatures were ubiquitous in the hedgerows and always struck her as so busy, scrambling here and there on their tiny legs.

"What a wonderful name!" She determined there and then to have a talking woodlouse called Mrs. Cheeseybob in her story.

It occurred to her she might bring her Tahiti book along with her and see if it interested the children who stopped to talk to her. The next day she read the story and showed the pictures to two of them. The day after, they were back with two more, and the day after that, with another. Soon she had a daily group sitting on the grass around her listening with open mouths to the story of Pierre, the twelve-year-old cabin boy who set sail for Polynesia.

"An those mens wears just them skirts tied around?" asked one of them. "Ain't they got no breeches?"

"It's hot there, so I suppose those skirts are more comfortable. Different people in different places wear different clothes, you know. It's cold and rainy here so we wear clothes to keep us warm. In Tahiti they wear clothes to keep them cool."

They readily agreed that this made perfect sense.

In fact, the autumn weather was at that time still quite warm, once the early morning mist had burned off. Still, Ellie wondered if there was somewhere she could read to the children regularly once the cooler days set in. Farrell Court would be over an hour's walk for most of them. She would have to ask Fletcher.

Chapter Twenty Six

But before the Marchioness could give any more thought to where she might set up a reading place for the children of the estate, fate intervened.

Back in London, Richard Forsythe, the handsome but rather effete typesetter at the publishing House of Woolstone & Browne had not forgotten the engaging Miss Maxwell who had come to them with her children's book.

"I say, sir, look at this!" he said one day about two weeks after the wedding of the Marquess of Hastings and Elisabeth Maxwell.

He approached his senior with the *London Gazette* in his hand. Mr. Woolstone (there was no longer a Mr. Browne; that gentleman had passed away some ten years before and lived only in memory) looked up at his employee in some degree of irritation. He had undertaken to edit a book written by a Ceylon tea merchant, the younger son of one of the Members of Parliament. That gentleman had returned to England after a career in tea that had ruined his health while lining his pockets but thinly. It was hoped the sale of a book written by someone so closely associated with government might plump up those pockets. But the man was a poor writer and the material so dry (how many more hundredweight of *camellia sinensis* could the reader be expected to read about?) that Mr. Woolstone was beginning to wish he had never taken on the task.

"What is it, Forsythe?"

"That lady—Miss Maxwell—who came here with the children's book about Tahiti. She's married the Marquess of Hastings!"

In fact, Mr. Forsythe had followed with interest the story of the Marquess's advertisement for a wife and subsequent announcement that a suitable candidate had been found. Mr. Sanderson had waited a week then put a brief announcement in the Court Circular to announce that the wedding of His Lordship the Sixth Marquess of Hastings to Elisabeth Mary Maxwell had taken place at a private ceremony. Mr. Forsythe had recognized the name immediately and now told his senior the whole story.

"You don't say!" Mr. Woolstone sat bolt upright. This was something like! "As I recall, the book might have had merit, but we couldn't undertake another children's book without money behind it. But if she's got a name, and better still a name with a little notoriety attached to it, well, that's a different kettle of fish!" He pondered a moment. "Look up the address of the Marquess of Hastings. It'll be in the *Peerage*."

So it was that a letter to the Marchioness of Hastings was sent to Farrell House in London, and made its way in due course up to Farrell Court.

Unaware that her dreams of publishing her little book were on their way to being fulfilled, Ellie came downstairs one morning in one of her new walking gowns ready to drive out in the gig. But the hall was vacant. She discovered later that one of the kitchen maids had burned her hand by picking up a large kettle of water just off the fire. She had let go of the vessel immediately and spilled its boiling contents all over the kitchen floor. Luckily no one had been seriously hurt, for they all wore stout boots, but the girl had set up such a howl that the butler and footmen had rushed downstairs. Her hand had been treated with a salve and bandaged up, and she was now in the housekeeper's room, sobbing as much from shock as anything. Cook, however, was in a fit over her flooded floor and all hands were on deck swabbing it up.

Up in her room, Ellie had heard nothing, and finding no one in the hall, decided to go to the stables herself and order the gig. As she came around the corner of the house she could see a group of men with their backs towards her, looking on as a large horse mounted the hind quarters of a smaller one and began pushing what looked like a stiff pipe between its rear legs. She stopped in confusion, and then, as the reality of what she had seen burst upon her, turned, her cheeks burning, and strode quickly back towards the front of the house. Her father's estate had not boasted many horses, and certainly no breeding. Besides, she had grown up mostly in town with her mother. She had never seen animals in the act of what she instinctively knew was copulation. Was this an image of what men and women did? Her shock gave way to a sense of dread, and it was some time before she gained enough control over her emotions to mount the steps back into the house and ask Prewitt to call for the gig. Then, because she didn't want to disappoint the children, she set out as she usually did. But instead of concentrating on the cheeseybobs, all she could see in her mind's eye was the vision of the two horses.

It was when she returned for lunch that day that the butler gave her the letter forwarded from London. Mr. Woolstone, of Woolstone & Browne, had written to her as follows:

Woolstone & Browne
Grub Street, London
The twelfth of October

Dear Lady Hastings,

Please allow me to felicitate you on your recent wedding and to convey my best wishes for your future happiness.

That happiness will, I hope, be augmented when I tell you that we have reconsidered your application to have your delightful little children's book published under our auspices. I hope you will remember my saying that it was the state of the market, not the quality of your work, which prevented our previous acceptance of it. I'm glad to say that things have turned around in that respect, and we can now see a ready readership for your book.

Please let me know when we may wait on you to discuss this further.

I remain, dear Lady Hasting, your most obedient servant,

Reginald Woolstone

Ellie's hands dropped to her lap as she considered this most unexpected missive. While she was in many ways a very sensible woman, she had had few dealings with business men, or, to be direct about it, men whose business it was to sell themselves and their services. When she read that the market had changed, she believed it. Not once did it occur to her that it was the change in her name that had effected this *volte-face* on the part of the publisher. She was not to know that a book written by a plain Elisabeth Maxwell held no allure for the buying public, whereas a book written by a Marchioness, and one, moreover, who had aspired to that position by answering an advertisement in the newspapers, was a different thing altogether.

"Nothing could be better than a Marchioness," Mr. Woolstone had declared, "unless it's a notorious Marchioness." And he had rubbed his hands together as if anticipating the gold that would soon be falling into them.

Chapter Twenty-Seven

In her room after luncheon, Ellie considered the two revelations the day had brought. She still felt the remnants of the shock she had experienced that morning, but it was overlaid with the excitement that her dreams of publishing were to come true. She would go up to London immediately and meet with Mr. Woolstone. James had said she could go when she liked, or even stay there if she wanted. It would be pleasant to see her mother, and possibly even order her a new gown. She would be so happy to buy her mother a gift from money she had earned herself!

She spent the rest of the afternoon working on her *Life in The Country* book. She wanted to show it to the publisher as her next book. She had decided that the animals would introduce themselves and tell about their lives. She had written and illustrated the pages for the horses and some of the insects she had sketched, but it was incomplete, as she still needed to visit the pigs and, importantly, illustrate the Princess of Maylands. She had seen that magnificent lady in the pasture, but just as James had said, she was far too busy eating for any sort of communication. Nevertheless, she thought what she had done enough to show the publishers what she intended.

She looked ruefully at the drawer where the beginnings of her *Odd Boy* book lay. She hadn't had time to do any more sketches for it, but after her visit to Nanny had added the titles for more pages:

> Once when he was really cross he threw his dinner against the wall.

> And another time he snapped his cousin's fishing rods right in two.

His tutor and his papa were not pleased.

But then, HE LEARNED. When he was cross, he closed his eyes.

And counted to ten.

And didn't shout or throw ANYTHING.

He grew to be a fine Man.

And everyone loved him, even though he was still a little odd.

She knew how she was going to illustrate most of them, and could hardly wait to get on with it. It would be quite fun showing her boy breaking things! The one about his tutor and his papa not being pleased would show him rubbing his posterior. That would convey the message, but not be too serious. The *fine man* gave her pause for a moment, but then she thought a picture of him on the hay wain would do the trick. The only page she didn't know how to illustrate was the last one. But it would come.

At dinner that evening James was preoccupied. The farmers were saying it looked like rain and were anxious to harvest the last of the hay. However, the field in which it lay received less sunlight than the others and the plants were still less than fully developed. The harvest would provide better fodder if the field could be left to grow another few days or even a week. On the other hand, it would rot if reaped when wet. He therefore listened with only half an ear when his wife told him about the letter from the publisher and asked if he would have any objection to her going to London for a few days.

"London?" he said with alarm. "I can't go."

"No, not you, me," replied Ellie patiently. "I should like to go and I don't mind going alone. I can stay with my mother and stepfather."

"Of course, as you wish." James was already back to thinking about the rain.

When Ellie told Mrs. Simmins she was going to London and would stay with her mother, the housekeeper looked surprised. After a moment's hesitation she said, "I hope you will not mind my mentioning it, my lady, but unless you have important reasons for not staying at Farrell House, I fear the staff there will be most distressed. Like us, they have waited so long for a new Lady Hastings, and would be very disappointed to know you were in London and not to see you there. They will think you dislike the place and them."

Remembering the elegant drawing room, Ellie exclaimed, "Oh no! Far from it! I think it's lovely, and Jessop the butler was extremely helpful. But It seems such a waste, opening up the whole house just for me!"

"And for whom should they open it up, if not for Lady Hastings?" replied Mrs. Simmins tartly. "And since his lordship despises the capital, if you do not go there, no one will."

"I hadn't thought of that!" said Ellie.

"Then, if you agree, I shall write a note to Mr. Jessop and inform him you will be there in, say, five days. That should give them enough time."

Ellie nodded her agreement and the thing was decided. She wrote letters to both her mother and Mr. Woolstone making arrangements to see them both. Then she was in a fever of excitement over the next few days.

The day before she was due to leave, she asked the maid who now routinely brought her breakfast in bed to bring up a bag for her trip, and the next thing she knew, Mrs. Simmins was in her bedchamber with a footman carrying her empty trunk.

"But I shan't need a whole trunk for a few days in London!" cried Ellie.

"A few days, my lady? I think not," replied the housekeeper. "As soon as the word is out that you are in the capital, you will find yourself engaged for several weeks with invitations. Everyone will want to meet the new Lady Hastings. I should count on a month, at least."

"Invitations? A month? Good heavens! I had never considered any of that! Are you sure?"

"Most certainly. No one will want to be backward in welcoming you. If what I have heard is true (for the London housekeeper Mrs. Varilly and she had kept up a lively correspondence and Mrs. Simmins knew all about the infamous advertisement), you will be the object of a good deal of interest. And I have decided that Lucy, the maid who has been looking after you, shall come with you. You cannot travel alone. She is young but not without sense, if she can be persuaded not to giggle. Once you are in London you may ask Mrs. Varilly to interview some dressers for you. And if I may say, my lady, since you have no one else to advise you, you will need some new gowns."

"But I just received some!"

"Oh, that was just a couple of walking suits and a day dress. Nothing to speak of. The *modiste* you have used seems excellent. You should go to see her as soon as may be and order more of everything."

"Gracious!" Ellie plumped down on her settee. "I had no idea!"

"Oh yes, my lady. The House of Hastings has at long last a new mistress, and she will be the center of a good deal of attention."

The following morning Ellie rose early to say goodbye to her husband at the breakfast table. He surprised her by saying, "I sent a note to the landlord of The Red Lion, where we ate on the way here. They are expecting you for luncheon. Timothy the driver knows. And I understand you will be staying at Farrell House, after all. They will be glad to see you. Mrs. Simmins and Mrs. Varilly have been in touch, so there should be no problem. If there is, speak to..."

Ellie interrupted with a smile, "Jessop. Yes, I understand. Butlers know everything!"

James smiled back. "Well, goodbye then," he said, and surprised her even more by coming forward and kissing her on the cheek. "I hope you enjoy yourself in London."

And he was gone.

Ellie put her hand to her cheek, warm with the blush she knew must be there. Her husband had never been that close to her before, and the combination of his soft lips and his masculine smell, a combination of soap and something like woodsmoke, had made her catch her breath. It was a moment or two before she was able to walk steadily upstairs to put on her bonnet and cloak. She took her reticule with the precious hundred pounds that Mr. Sanderson had sent, pulled on her gloves and went down to get into the carriage.

Chapter Twenty-Eight

The journey to London was uneventful except for the explosions of happiness from Lucy the maid who had never been away from home before. She thought the very grass was greener and the sky bluer the closer they got to the capital. The meal she was served at the Red Lion, where she ate with the driver and groom, while her ladyship dined in splendid isolation, was, according to her, done to a cow's thumb. It was heaven on earth for her to be seated at a table with a cloth, and be served her food like a queen. This she explained to her ladyship in great detail when they resumed their journey, before falling asleep with her mouth open.

The arrival at the London house was equal to what Ellie had received at Farrell Court. The journey from there to Mayfair had been made so many times over the years, that the servants knew to within half an hour what time to expect her. As soon as the groom pulled the doorbell, the hall was filled with the servants waiting to greet their new mistress. She knew Jessop, of course, and felt she knew Mrs. Varilly after her name being mentioned so often, but she despaired of remembering all the others. She had only just learned the names of the servants at Farrell Court. But they greeted her warmly and seemed prepared to love her, so she smiled and gave what answers she could to their questions about her journey, how his lordship was going on in the country and when they might expect to see him.

After dining again in splendid isolation, Ellie went down to the kitchens to thank the cook. She felt shy doing so on her own, but told herself that she might be more blamed for being haughty than for being friendly. They were certainly surprised to see her, but when she went back upstairs they were loud in her praise.

"Very nice lady, she is, to be sure," was the common opinion. "Not too high. She's a good match for his lordship, for all his way of getting a wife was peculiar." Because of course, they all knew about the newspaper advertisement.

Her ladyship went up the stairs to her bedchamber. She had been taken there when she first arrived and had found a spacious room furnished in much the same style as her apartment at Farrell Court. The late Lady Hastings must have made that her particular style. It was comfortable, feminine and welcoming. The draperies were less faded than those at Maylands, probably because the room received less afternoon sun, and the soft pink was very pleasing. Her trunk had been unpacked and her nightgown was folded on her bed. She sank gratefully into her bed, and as she fell asleep, brought her hand to the spot her husband had kissed that morning.

As Mrs. Simmins had foretold, the minute the word was out that the new Lady Hastings was in residence, Ellie was besieged with visiting cards and invitations. How the *ton* had ascertained this information was a mystery to her, since no notice had been put in the Court Circular to inform the world of her presence in the capital.

When she expressed her surprise to Mrs. Varilly, that lady laughed and said, "Oh, it will have been one of the servants dropping a casual word here or there. That is the best way in this town for disseminating information."

"If I refuse the invitations I shall appear churlish," sighed Ellie, but if I accept, I cannot possibly reciprocate unless I stay here for months." And, surprised as she was to discover it, that was not an attractive thought. She was missing her life in the country: the rides, sketching, the children, and yes, most of all, her husband.

"We could hold a dinner to respond to many invitations at once, but in the absence of his lordship, that would be difficult. Unless, my lady," said the housekeeper, "you have another gentleman who could stand in for him. Your stepfather, perhaps?" Mrs. Varilly said this with obvious doubt in her voice. Word of Mr. Brownlow's demeanor at Grillon's after the wedding had made its way back to Farrell House.

"Oh, no!" replied Ellie at once. Memories of the awkward dinner parties she had endured with him had not faded. "That is, I... I wouldn't feel comfortable doing it without my husband." But they both knew what she meant.

Mrs. Varilly was eager to open up Farrell House in some way and was determined not to let this opportunity pass. In the early days of the late Marquess' marriage, they had held balls and dinners, post-opera suppers and concert evenings, but nothing like that had been done for over twenty years.

"Then if I may suggest, my lady," replied the housekeeper, "we should hold an *at home* for the ladies. Their opinion is anyway more important than the gentlemen's, and the absence of his lordship would not be felt."

Like Mrs. Simmins, Mrs. Varilly was a motherly creature and had been with the family since before James was born. Ellie felt no compunction in displaying her ignorance.

"That is a good idea!" she said, "but I have no experience of hosting such a thing."

"Not to worry," smiled the housekeeper. "All you will have to do is smile and greet the ladies. Mr. Jessop and I will do the rest!"

So for every invitation Ellie received, Lady Hastings responded with one for an *at home* to be held shortly before her departure.

She could not accept every offer of entertainment delivered through her door. Balls were out of the question, with no gentleman to partner her. She knew that even married ladies often attended dances with an unexceptional single gentleman or *cicisbeo*, the sort everyone knew to be a confirmed bachelor. But she knew none of them, and would have had no desire to go, even if she had. It occurred to her she had never danced with her husband. *Did* he dance, she wondered? Neither would she accept an invitation to a masquerade at the Vauxhall Gardens. Her mother had always told her these were not the venue for a lady and often dissolved into a mad romp.

She did, however, accept invitations to dinner, to musical evenings and to soirées described as *just a quiet evening with friends.* These generally turned out to be anything but quiet, with all sorts of games and inexpert renditions on the pianoforte by debutantes being shown off by their mamas. Not many remembered her from her entrance into society under the aegis of Lady Penhale, who, at her age, was no longer often seen at tonnish parties. Everyone knew the Marquess had found her through an advertisement in the newspaper. At first she was conscious of being regarded rather as one might regard a monkey: not knowing which way it would jump. But before long she gained a reputation for being a very pretty-behaved young woman, beautifully dressed, with pleasing manners and good conversation.

"Don't know how Jim did it," was the assessment of one of his old school friends. "Never saw him with a woman in m'life and he finds the perfect one. Amazin'!"

Ellie spent several days with her mother, who was in tears of joy to see her daughter delivered to her door in an emblazoned carriage and looking every bit a Lady. She went to her *modiste,* who was delighted to make as many gowns for the young Marchioness as she wanted. Since Ellie had been very open with the name of the person who clothed her so beautifully, Hélène was already beginning to receive new commissions and a new junior seamstress was being kept very busy with seam and hem sewing.

She invited her mother and Mr. Brownlow to a quiet family dinner at Farrell House. As he stepped into the elegant townhouse, her stepfather tried to act as if to the manner born, but gave himself away by trying to find out the price of everything he saw. Since Ellie couldn't help him with any of it, he was about to ask Jessop, when his wife, conscious not of her own position but of her daughter's, said warningly *Mr. Brownlow!* and frowned awfully at him. He forbore.

But her most anticipated visit was to Woolstone & Browne, the publishers. When she arrived at the premises, she was ushered in and seated as reverently as if she had been royalty. She was offered tea, which she declined.

"My lady," intoned Mr. Woolstone, as he carefully turned the pages of her Tahiti book, in marked contrast to the way in which he had carelessly flipped through them the last time, "may I say how beautiful your work is, and how fortunate any young person will be to receive a copy."

In fact, he had hardly taken any note of her exquisite illustrations and charming text. Anything written by the notorious Marchioness would sell, and he knew it.

"I brought the first pages of a new book I'm working on," said Ellie, showing him her *Life In The Country* pages.

The publisher barely glanced at them. "Charming, charming!" he said. "Let us see how well the first book goes, but I see no reason why we should not be delighted to take this as soon as it is ready."

"You don't object to talking cows and woodlice, then, Mr. Woolstone?"

"Cows and... and wood, er woodlice?" Then he realized she was talking about her new book. He didn't care if it was talking haystacks so long as it came from the pen of an author who would sell. "Of course, of course, delightful!" he answered. "Just the thing for the kiddies! And may I say how the name of the illustrious House of Hastings will be further burnished by your accomplishment." He handed the pages back to her.

Ellie, busy putting them away, said absently, "But I have written them under my maiden name, you know."

The publisher made no reply, but if she had been looking up instead of down at her bag, she would have seen him raise his eyebrows.

Mr. Forsythe, the typesetter, could hardly take his eyes off their visitor. His heart had been touched by Ellie when she was a penniless author, and he had thought now she was a great lady, he would find her changed. Not so. Apart from the fact she was beautifully gowned, she was still the same. She greeted him warmly as an old acquaintance, spoke to him as an equal and was genuinely interested in the printing process he explained to her. By the time she left, with promises from Mr. Woolstone that he would be in touch very soon, his heart was fully hers. He imagined her in a remote castle with a boorish but wealthy husband who had only married her because he wanted an heir. He wanted to save her.

Chapter Twenty-Nine

Everyone agreed the *at home* given by the Marchioness of Hastings was a delightful affair. The townhouse looked beautiful, decorated by massed late blooming white roses with orange and gold chrysanthemums. Ellie, her mother and Mrs. Varilly had visited a florist in Chelsea and had been assured of a vast delivery of his finest blooms on the day of the *at home*. With cook they also discussed appropriate comestibles that would be served all afternoon as visitors came and went.

"It isn't a tea party," said her ladyship, "so if we serve a champagne cup instead of tea, we can offer little savory tartlets as well as fruit ones, with other sweetmeats, of course. And I should like there to be *plenty* of everything. I want people to think well of the House of Hastings."

The cook and housekeeper exchanged smiling glances. It did their hearts good to hear this sentiment from their new mistress. Mrs. Brownlow glowed with pride.

The champagne cup proved very popular with the guests. A few of the ladies went tipsily to their carriages declaring they had never so much enjoyed an *at home*. The young Marchioness, with her ready conversation and open, charming manner was declared a superior hostess.

Just two days after this triumph, Ellie returned to Maylands. With her in the carriage were both Lucy the maid and her newly employed dresser. Ellie had not been persuaded of the need for such a person until Mrs. Varilly explained that now her ladyship had such an extensive wardrobe, it was too much for either her or Mrs. Simmins to look after it all. Hearing that, the Marchioness readily agreed, asking only they hire someone who could manage her hair.

She was accustomed to pinning it up in the simplest way, with the result it tended to tumble down during the day. She was realizing more every day what Mr. Sanderson had meant by *standards*.

They tested this requirement by having each of the candidates do her ladyship's hair. Of the three candidates chosen as the most suitable, it was Grace Baxter, a woman not much older than Ellie herself, who proved most adept. She swept up the Marchioness's curls with complete assurance and performed a miraculous coiffure with apparently just the flick of her wrist. She did up her mistress's hair for the *at home* with such expertise that it looked beautiful all afternoon. Now she was looking all around as they left London, calmly delighted at the prospect of a sojourn in the country. Lucy the maid had at first been jealous of her mistress's new attendant, but the dresser had a friendly disposition and did not lord it over those inferior to herself in the domestic hierarchy, so they were soon in perfect agreement.

They arrived at Farrell Court towards teatime, and Ellie was once again struck by the tranquility that reigned over the place. The late autumn sun was low in the sky, throwing a cloak of gold over the old bricks and reflecting like flame in the many tall windows. She went upstairs to her apartment which awaited her, warm and honey-colored, and greeted her like an old friend. The footmen brought up her trunks—two of them now she had an expanded wardrobe—and Grace put her things away. Lucy brought her a cup of tea and a plate of macaroons, with the message that cook had made them specially for her return. She was home.

Ellie was dozing on her settee when the five o'clock bell rang. Grace helped her into one of her new evening gowns, a ruby velvet creation with a creamy satin underskirt that made her skin glow. She re-did her ladyship's coiffure, tumbled from the nap on the settee, and sent her forth, looking radiant. Ellie went downstairs to await the arrival of her husband, to be told that he was already upstairs with his valet.

He came striding into the drawing room a few minutes later, a smile on his face. "Elisabeth! I'm so pleased you're back! I've missed talking to you over dinner." He took her outstretched hand and bowed over it. He made no comment on her new gown, or her coiffure, instead burst out with, "I've so much to tell you! The rain held off and we were able to finish the last harvest. More than twice the yield of last year! The Princess is now nearly six hundred pounds! I'm hopeful of breeding her in another month or so. She's magnificent!"

"Hello, James," laughed Ellie, "It's good to see you too. But it seems as if you've told me everything already. It sounds as if I shall need to draw another picture of the Princess. She must be even fatter than before."

"She certainly is, and ..." as they walked into dinner, he continued with his recitation of hundredweights, tonnages and turnips in a way that Mr. Woolstone, had he been there to hear it, would have found very dull indeed. Ellie knew her husband by now, and if in her heart she would have preferred to be welcomed home with another kiss on the cheek, or even a kiss on the hand, she didn't take the recitation amiss.

Life resumed as it had been before. The fine weather was holding, even though they were into mid-October. The mornings were cool and the sun was setting earlier, but for long periods of the day it was still warm enough for her to sketch outside and read to the children.

Her relationship with her husband stayed exactly the same. He was perfectly friendly, told her about his days and listened to what she said about hers; he laughed at the same things she did, and genuinely seemed to enjoy her company. But it went no further. He never again kissed her on the cheek, and Ellie began to wonder what had made him do it that one time. She wondered if she should kiss him, but that went against everything she had been taught. Gentlemen were supposed to take the lead in such things. She didn't know what to do. She wondered if she should consult Nanny, but recoiled at exposing such intimate thoughts to a third party. So she simply continued as before. She worked a great deal on her books, both the *Life In The Country* and *The Life of An Odd Boy.* She completed the first and almost finished the second, but still didn't know how to illustrate the last page.

Chapter Thirty

About a month after her return to the country, she received a package from Woolstone & Browne containing not the proofs of her Tahiti book, but a published copy. The little book was very nicely done and finely bound. Her heart leaped when she saw it, as any author's must. But dismay overcame her joy when she saw the title page. She had written it under her maiden name, and that's how it had been given to the publisher. But he had replaced that with her married name and title, and in large type, so no one could miss it.

Pierre the Cabin Boy's Voyage to Tahiti

Being the Diary of a Boy's Trip to the Polynesian Island

And his Many Curious Observations

By

Her Ladyship Elisabeth Farrell,

Marchioness of Hastings

Ellie was horrified. It had never been her intention to capitalize on her husband's name. She knew his family was already infuriated by the unwelcome publicity caused by his advertisement for a wife. Now this! To see it plastered all over the front of bookshop windows! But perhaps it wouldn't sell any copies, perhaps no one would ever see it.

She wrote to the publishers expressing her severe displeasure and asking why she had never seen the promised proofs, when she would have prevented her husband's name being associated with this venture. Mr. Woolstone replied.

> *My dear Lady Hastings,*
>
> *I write this prostrate with grief at the idea I may have acted wrongly. Alas! One cannot trust even the most valued of employees. I was under the misapprehension that my assistant, Mr. Forsythe had indeed sent you proofs and all was accepted. I very much regret to tell you it is now Too Late. Copies have already been widely distributed and according to reports, the volume is selling very well. That well-known institution The Temple of the Muses has today ordered a further fifty copies and we have received requests from as far afield as Manchester and Edinburgh. I hope the knowledge that you have taken the town by storm will help assuage any misgivings you may feel. You will receive a cheque from us in due course.*
>
> *Your most obedient servant,*
> *Reginald Woolstone*

It was a complete lie, of course. Mr. Woolstone had never intended to send the proofs to Elisabeth. He had made that decision the minute she had mentioned writing under her maiden name. He had not made any comment at the time, with a businessman's intuition that the fewer the questions, the better for business. Richard Forsythe knew nothing of the matter and had been only slightly surprised when the author had made no changes at all to the proofs. For him, the setting of the book had been a labor of love and he was sure there were no errors and no one could have done it better.

That evening Ellie decided to make a clean breast of it all to her husband.

"James, you remember the book I was writing when I met you in *The Temple of the Muses?*"

"The one about de Bougainville and Tahiti?"

"Yes. Well, it's been published and it's selling quite well, apparently." She scowled.

"Why are you scowling? Isn't that what you wanted?"

"Yes, but... but the thing is, I wrote it under my maiden name, and they've published it under my married name and title. Now I think about it, I'm sure they only wanted it because of that. I'm so sorry."

"Why should you be sorry? The family's been known for some damned—excuse me—for some very stupid things over the years. M' grandfather's name is in the book at White's for every idiotic wager you can imagine. How many minutes it would take to get down Pall Mall in a wheelbarrow; how many glasses of burgundy he could balance on a piece of toast between two books; you've no idea. And you know how my uncle and cousin feel about the advertisement in the newspaper. If the name can withstand that, it can withstand a very nice book with Hastings on the front."

"But they're bound to think I only did it to take advantage of the name, and truly, I didn't."

"The *ton* already think I'm dicked in the nob, so it won't make any difference. We'll just stay in the country and they can say what they like."

"Oh, James, you are so sweet! Thank you!"

Before she had time to think about it, she ran around the table and kissed him on the cheek. He looked up at her with an odd look in his eyes and seemed about to say something, but did not. Ellie stood there, a blush rising in her cheeks, not knowing quite what to do. Then she said gruffly, "Well, anyway...," and went back to her seat. They finished their meal almost in silence, then James went to visit his Princess and Ellie went up to her room, to think, and yes, to cry a little. It had obviously been a mistake to kiss her husband. She saw that now. He hadn't known what to do or say. How embarrassing for both of them!

The next few days were difficult. James was preoccupied and Ellie didn't know how to approach him. Their dinner conversation concentrated on nothing more than the fine weather they were still enjoying, punctuated by long silences. In the end, to take her mind off the whole affair, she decided to visit the Princess and see how much bigger she had become. She had already completed a page for her in the new book, but it might be amusing to do another sketch putting a butterfly or a grasshopper on the end of her nose and thus showing how large she was. Besides, this would give her and her husband something to talk about. She asked for the gig and drove herself to the pasture where she knew the heifer would be.

There she was, a magnificent brown and white animal, with a head that looked small compared with the very large body. Ellie drew the gig to a halt, took her little stool and sketch pad, and opened the gate into the field and closed it behind her, leaving the pony cropping the grass on the verge. As James had said, the

Princess was far too interested in eating to pay any attention to this strange visitor, and continued chewing.

Ellie sat there for two hours working on different angles to best capture the heifer, and wishing a real butterfly would land on her nose. It was hard to get the dimensions right. She was just starting to get a little chilly, for the sun was beginning to go down, when she heard the voices of children next to her gig. She hastily gathered up her belongings and left the pasture. She was in a hurry to see the children and as she came out of the gate, she dropped her stool, then, in picking it up, dropped her sketch book. They came swarming around her to help.

"'Ave you got your book, m'lady, about the cabin boy 'n Teetee," asked one of the boys, a lad of about seven who was enthralled with the idea of going on a boat. He had never seen the sea, and the only boats in his experience were the row boats used for fishing on the estate ponds and rivers. The idea of sleeping in a hammock while the boat sailed over the waves filled his imagination.

"No, because I gave it to a publisher in London who has made lots of copies of it. I'll ask him to send me enough for you all to have one."

"'Ave one for me very own?" the lad's eyes were round.

"Yes, then you can tell the story yourself to the little ones at home." All the families had large numbers of children and she guessed there were little ones. About his ability to tell the story, she didn't need to guess. He had memorized every line.

She chatted with the children for a while longer, then climbed into the gig and drove home. She settled down to color her image of the Princess. She worked quietly, losing all sense of time, when suddenly she heard steps pounding up the stairs. Her sitting room door was flung open and James stood there, thunder in his face.

"You idiot!" he shouted. "You left the Princess's gate open and the bull got at her! An undersized young bull, put out to fatten him up! She was just ready for mating! I've been thinking and thinking about which one to put her with for the best size calf. I can't believe it! He was the worst! The last one I would have chosen! Nearly a year's work ruined!"

He strode up and down the room like a caged animal.

"I... I... *did* I?" Ellie was stunned. "I think I closed it, really I do!"

"It had to be you! The men say they saw you in the field. No countryperson would be stupid enough to leave a gate open!"

Ellie was trying to remember. She could see herself closing the gate on the way into the pasture, but on the way out, with dropping everything, it was a blur. All she could see was the children, and talking to them about her book. Had she left the gate unlatched? It was possible.

But her husband was still shouting at her. "You with your pencils and papers and your head full of stories! I should never have let you near the Princess! And filling the children with idiotic notions about sailing across the sea! They will be farmers like their fathers and their fathers' fathers before them! They need common sense, not your faradiddle!"

This made Ellie angry. She could understand having a peal rung over her for leaving the gate open. She knew that a closed gate was the farmer's friend. But to be criticized for telling the children stories, for opening their minds to different experiences, that she would not tolerate. She sprang to her feet.

"Just because they are destined to be farmers, doesn't mean they are destined to be ignorant!" she shouted back. "I'm sorry about your Princess, but after all, she is just a cow! And if a bull mated with her, they were only doing what nature intended." And before she could stop herself, the words tumbled out. "Which is more than happens in this house! I could find it in myself to be jealous of the Princess! That bull has a good deal more gumption than you! You haven't had gates closed against you, but you haven't taken advantage of it, not for a moment!"

She regretted the words as soon as they were out of her mouth, but it was too late. Her husband stopped his enraged stalking up and down and stared at her. There was complete silence in the room for about ten seconds, then James turned on his heel and left her.

Ellie sank down onto her settee, covering her mouth with her hand. Her heart was pounding and for several moments was unable to think at all. Then she was horrified. Whatever had come over her? How could she have said that? What was she to do now? Her breath coming in gasps, she knew there was only one thing to do. She couldn't face her husband ever again. She must leave.

Chapter Thirty-One

Prewitt was astonished when her ladyship came into the hall and told him to call the carriage. She was going to London.

"London, my lady? At this time of day?"

"Yes. Kindly do as I ask without delay."

"And his lordship...?" The butler had heard loud voices from upstairs, and though he hadn't heard what was said, he knew it was enough to make the Marquess come down the stairs looking like a man possessed and stride out of the front door without looking to left or right.

"Oh no, he will not be coming. He's too busy here. Anyway, enough of this talking. Please call the carriage immediately."

Ellie ran back upstairs to find her dresser in her room, taking an evening gown out of the cupboard.

"No, Grace," she said, shortly. "My traveling gown and cloak, please. I am going to London."

And as the other woman looked at her in surprise, she said, "No questions. You may put my nightclothes and a day dress into a bag. That is all I shall need. If I need more, I'll let you know and you may send it."

"I send it, my lady? But I shall come with you, of course."

"That won't be necessary"

"May I ask if his lordship taking his valet?"

"I am going alone."

This was said with such finality that Grace dared make no answer. She packed a bag as directed and in less than half an hour, her ladyship was driving up the gravel path away from Farrell Court, vowing never to return. She had brought with her the material for her *Life in the Country* book, except for the latest image of the Princess which was unfinished and which she hoped, anyway, never to lay eyes on again. She would spend the night at her mother's and tomorrow go to Woolstone & Browne. She would persuade them to produce her second book and in the meantime live on the proceeds from the first. The whole marriage to the Marquess of Hastings had been ridiculous from the start. She had allowed herself to be carried away on the wings of hope and her own imagination. In that respect, at least her husband was right. Her head was full of stories.

At the Red Lion she told the coachman to simply change horses and keep going. She did not stop for dinner, or even a cup of tea. By the time they arrived in London, it was gone ten and it was fully dark. The gas lamps were lit and casting fantastic shadows that reflected the nightmare in her mind. She directed the driver to take her to her mother's home and then go to Farrell House for the night. They should return to the country tomorrow and pick up his lordship's horses on the way.

The coachman would not leave, however, until the groom had pulled the doorbell and seen it opened by Mr. Brownlow's astonished butler. Mr. and Mrs. Brownlow were from home, he said, but Miss Maxwell, er, beg pardon, her ladyship was welcome to come in. Ellie was glad she would not have to explain herself immediately to either her mother or her stepfather. She asked only that a cup of tea and a piece of bread and butter be brought to her room, and having consumed them, fell wearily into bed. She was asleep when her mother tapped at her door around midnight.

"I am sure," said Mrs. Brownlow to her husband, who was full of questions about their unexpected visitor, "it is merely because

Elisabeth did not want to open up Farrell House for a short visit. I'm delighted she feels she is still welcome here, are not you, Mr. Brownlow?"

Faced with a question to which there was only one acceptable answer, he grumpily agreed. "But I don't see why I have to feed and house her when her husband is rich as... as...," he knew there was a king or something that rich people were compared to, but for the life of him, he couldn't remember who it was. "As rich as anything," he ended weakly.

The following morning at the breakfast table Ellie readily agreed with the excuse fabricated by her mother and said she would only be there a day or two. She said nothing about leaving her husband, only explaining she was going to see her publishers.

"Of course, yes!" exclaimed her mother. "One sees your little book wherever one goes. Just the other day I was passing *The Temple of the Muses* and saw in a display in the front of their window. Whoever would have thought it? I hope you have reserved a copy for us!"

"I shall make sure they send you one," promised Ellie. "I had no idea it would be so popular. Mr. Woolstone tells me it has even been requested in Scotland and the provinces!"

"A good earner, I expect," said Mr. Brownlow, who had forgotten his criticism of his stepdaughter now he saw there was money in being a bluestocking. "How much have they paid you?"

When Ellie said she had received nothing yet, but had been promised a cheque, Mr. Brownlow harrumphed and said she hoped she knew what she was doing without a man to guide her. He made noises about accompanying her, which was the last thing she wanted, so as soon as she could, she slipped out of the house and took a hackney to Woolstone & Browne.

It turned out that Mr. Woolstone was at home with a putrid sore throat. His assistant Mr. Forsythe was, however, delighted to see the object of the fantasies inhabiting his dreams.

"My lady," he said, kissing her hand fervently. "I dared not hope to see you so soon! The capital is indeed embellished by your presence! I hold myself in readiness to be of whatever service I may be to you."

Ellie was a little surprised at the fulsomeness of his remarks, but answered in her practical way, "If I may, I should like to know how much I may expect to… to receive from my first book. I am thinking, you see, of finding a small place where I may pursue my artistic endeavors without bothering my husband." This, at least, was mostly true.

"I comprehend you entirely, my dear lady Hastings," replied the besotted young man. "It must be difficult indeed to live a life of the mind when forced to endure the animal appetites of the person upon whom one is dependent."

Ellie thought the comment rather strange, but let it pass. Mr. Forsythe disappeared for a few minutes and returned with a cheque which he gave to Ellie.

"I do not like to deal with such a lovely lady as yourself with such gross commercialism," he said, "but Mr. Woolstone had prepared this to send to you before his unfortunate illness".

He handed her a cheque for two hundred and fifty pounds. Ellie looked at it in astonishment. "Good gracious!" she cried. "That is a great deal of money!"

"No more than you deserve, dear lady," said her admirer. "You have taken the town by storm. I daresay there is not a household in London, and now in the provinces, where they do not wish to own a copy. We are going into a second edition."

"I'm delighted to hear it, "she said, "because I've brought the material for a second book that I hoped Mr. Woolstone would consider." She handed him the portfolio of *Life In The Country*.

Mr. Forsythe opened it with reverence, as one might an ancient Bible, and let out a sigh of wonder. "It is altogether perfect!" he exclaimed after a moment or two. "The concept is novel and the illustrations exquisite. I think I may safely say Mr. Woolstone will take it on." After the success of *Pierre The Cabin Boy*, he knew his senior would leap at a second book.

Ellie suddenly thought of her promise to her mother. "Please will you send a copy of *Pierre* to my mother, Mrs. Brownlow. Here is the direction." She quickly wrote it down and handed it him. Then she remembered her other promise. "And twenty copies to Farrell Court," she said, and hesitated. She would never see those children again, and certainly not be there to distribute the books. A lump came into her throat. She would write a note to Mrs. Simmins who would surely do it for her. But she could not control the tears that came to her eyes as she thought about the children. She groped in her reticule for a handkerchief.

"My lady!" Mr. Forsythe ran to her side and knelt beside her. "Pray do not upset yourself!" Then his emotions overcame him. He grasped her hands and his words rushed out. "How I feel for your situation and how I have longed these last months, to be able to rescue you! I have thought of nothing else! I am a poor man, with naught but my skills to support me, but with the income from your books, my dearest Elisabeth, we could go far away and live together secluded! A cottage, yes, just a cottage, humble in the view of the world, but an earthly paradise for us!"

He pulled an astonished Ellie to her feet, and before she could prevent him, planted hot kisses all over her face.

"Mr. Forsythe! Mr. Forsythe! You forget yourself, indeed you do," she protested, trying desperately to fend him off and thinking she must be dealing with a madman.

But in his passion he did not hear her. "Fly with me now, Elisabeth! Fly with me! You need not return to that monster! Let me protect you from him!"

Then a voice came from the doorway. "Well, the monster is here, and desires you to unhand his wife. She appears to need more protection from you than from him."

Ellie gave a great cry of relief, wrenched herself from the grip of the typesetter and threw herself onto the broad chest of her husband, James Farrell, sixth Marquess of Hastings.

Chapter Thirty-Two

When Ellie made her uncontrolled declaration back at Farrell Court, it had taken her husband a moment to comprehend what she meant. Then he strode from the room and from the house in such a fury he would have smashed everything and everyone in his path had he not, through long training, controlled himself. He set off at random, not knowing where he was going, muttering *only a cow, could find it in myself to be jealous, more gumption than you,* until he found himself going in the direction of Nanny's cottage. He rapped on her door in a way that she knew from long experience it was him, and he was in a rage about something.

"Don't get up!" he said as he came in, then threw himself into the chair opposite her by the fire.

She said nothing but waited for him to begin. It had always been best that way.

"She left the gate open and the bull got at my prize heifer," he said furiously and without preamble.

"You are talking of your wife, I collect," said Nanny, calmly. "Was it deliberate, do you think?"

"Of course not. She wouldn't do that." Even in his anger, James knew this was true.

"So it was a mistake. We all make those. You know that better than anyone, my lord."

"Oh don't bring all that up, Nanny. I damned well know I've made mistakes. But then she said… she said…," he had difficulty repeating everything his wife had said. "She said it was only natural."

"And so it is." She hesitated. "Will your heifer only ever bear one calf?"

"No. I hope to breed her in the future, naturally."

"So even though this... event may lead to a calf not exactly what you want, there is still time?"

"Yes, I suppose so." His lordship was calming down.

"So this is a temporary setback, at most. Tell me, my lord," said Nanny, looking directly into his eyes, "who is more important to you, the Princess or your wife?"

The question astonished him. It was one he had never asked himself. As he thought about it, he realized that if he'd been asked four months before, without a blink he would have answered *the Princess*. But now, he knew that was no longer true. His wife had become essential to his happiness. He raised his head and looked at his dear old Nanny. As usual, she had put her finger on the issue. "My wife," he said, simply.

"Then, my lord, you must go back and tell her so."

The Marquess leaped to his feet. "By God! I shall!" he cried. "Thank you, Nanny! And I've said it before. Stop calling me *my lord*!"

"But you are a Lord, James. Not in name only, but in character. I know I'm partial, but I think you will be the finest Marquess of Hastings yet. Now go home to your wife."

By the time he arrived back at Farrell Court, Ellie was gone. James did not realize this and went galloping up the stairs shouting "Elisabeth!" He was in her rooms before Prewitt caught up with him.

"Her ladyship called for the carriage and left almost two hours ago, my lord." The old butler hesitated then said tentatively, "I... I imagine she received word that something was amiss with her mother, and that made her leave so precipitously."

James stared at the butler. "No," he said. "We had an..." Then he remembered what Ellie had said about white lies. Sometimes they were better than the truth. "Er yes, of course, Prewitt. That's just it. A note from her mother. I hope the staff understands." And he looked at the old retainer meaningfully.

"Of course, my lord. Will you, er, will you be leaving also, or should I tell cook to serve dinner?"

"Ask cook to make me a sandwich. I'll eat it up here. And tell Furber to pack me a small bag. I'll be going alone."

"At once, my lord." The butler bowed his way out.

James wandered over to his wife's desk, where her new illustration of the Princess was half colored. He looked at it and smiled. It was charming. His huge heifer was shown, her head up for once, looking in a perplexed fashion at a butterfly on the end of her nose. The penciled-in text read:

"What are you?" asked the butterfly.

"I'm a prize heifer," said the Princess of Maylands. "I'm the biggest heifer in the County, perhaps in the land. I am going to have calves who will grow up to be even bigger than me."

"Oh, I thought you were a mountain," replied the butterfly. "I am very small and I shall have very small children. They won't look like me at first. They will start as tiny eggs that will grow into caterpillars. Then they will

make themselves a cocoon and when they break out, they will look like me."

Around the edge of the page were pencil drawings of the life cycle of the butterfly. James looked around for the other pages to the book, but could find none. He did, however, find another little book entitled *The Life of an Odd Boy.* He recognized himself immediately. But the drawings were done with such sympathy and gentle humor he couldn't possibly take offence. His heart filled when he saw them. His Elisabeth. She understood him. He had to get her back.

Half an hour later, he too was on the road. On his huge hunter he made good time and arrived at Farrell House less than an hour after Ellie had arrived at her mother's.

"Where is my wife?" he asked a surprised Jessop.

"Her ladyship, sir? I'm afraid I cannot tell you. I thought she was with you at Maylands."

"You mean she didn't come here?"

"No, my lord. Were we to expect her? We didn't receive any notice."

"Er, no. It was a last minute thing. Her mother is… er, ailing." Really, these white lies were easy once one got in the habit!

Just at that moment, a footman came into the hall to tell Jessop that the carriage had arrived from Maylands. Her ladyship had been taken to her mother's residence and the coachman and two grooms had been told to return to Maylands the next day.

"Tell them not to leave until I see them," said the Marquess, then turning to Jessop. "Have them saddle up another horse for me. I'm going to see my wife."

"Now, my lord? it's gone twelve. Surely her ladyship will have retired. She will be tired after the journey and if Mrs. Brownlow is ailing, such a disruption can do her no good. May I suggest you wait until morning? May I bring you some refreshment after your long ride, my lord?"

Annoyed he hadn't made up a different lie, James nevertheless agreed what Jessop said was true, agreed to have something to eat and finally took himself off to bed.

His rest was disturbed by thoughts of the Princess and her wholly unsuitable mate, and by contrast, of his Elisabeth who, he knew, was his wholly suitable mate. How could he have been so foolish? He tossed and turned and finally fell asleep in the early hours of the morning, with the result he slept later than he had intended. He leaped out of bed, rang for hot water and when it came, having performed his toilet, dressed himself. He sorely missed Furber, who would have done a much finer job with his neck cloth and made sure his boots had no thumb prints. For the first time in his life he wanted to make a good impression. He did the best he could, but there's no doubt his father would have found fault with his appearance. It was after eleven by the time he arrived at the Brownlow residence.

"I'm sorry, my lord," said his mother-in-law. "Was Ellie expecting you? She didn't say so. She has gone to her publishers. You know her book is all the rage of course? How proud we are of her. I'm sure you must be too. What are people at Maylands saying about it? But won't you come in and wait? I'm sure she cannot be long."

James was never at his best when peppered with questions, and on this occasion too distraught to even try to answer them all. But one thing he did not want was to wait. He said so, and abruptly took his leave.

"Who were you talking to?" said Mr. Brownlow, coming into the salon a few minutes later.

"It was the Marquess. He was looking for Ellie. How odd they didn't come to town together. But he *is* odd, there's no getting away from it. He didn't seem remotely interested in dear Ellie's book."

"Book? Why should he be interested?" answered her husband scornfully. "Books aren't a gentleman's business! And he's so plump in the pocket a few hundred here or there can make no difference whatever. But why didn't you offer him a glass of wine, my dear? I should have liked a chat with him about an idea I've got. I might be able to put a good thing his way."

"But I thought you said a few hundred here or there wouldn't make any difference to him," said his wife mildly.

"A few hundred? Pshaw! You think I'd talk to him about anything as paltry as that?"

Mrs. Brownlow reflected that not so long ago a few hundred would have made a very great difference indeed to her. She might not even have been encouraged to marry her husband. But she said nothing of that, of course.

Chapter Thirty-Three

Holding his wife to his chest in the offices of Woolstone & Browne, James felt an enormous relief. She had run to him. She wasn't going to leave him.

"You were right," he said, looking down at her. "She is only a cow. And I should have taken advantage of the open gate. That bull knew better than me. Let's go home."

Ellie burst into tears.

"Sir!" exclaimed the unfortunate Mr. Forsythe. "You tell me to unhand your wife, but the minute she is in your arms, she cannot forbear to weep!"

"No, no, you don't understand, Mr. Forsythe." Ellie half laughing, half crying. "I love him! I love my husband. He isn't any sort of monster. He's kind and funny and… I love him," she said for the third time.

"And I love you," said the Marquess, smiling down at his wife. "I love you, Ellie."

And he kissed her, full on the lips, a long, lingering kiss that Ellie wanted never to end. She put her arms around her husband's neck and would not let him go.

Richard Forsythe could no longer fool himself that he was looking at a maiden in distress. He was embarrassingly *de trop*. He turned and left the room.

Ellie and James rode home together, hand in hand, that afternoon. They had a great deal to say to each other, though neither knew where to start.

"Why didn't you... haven't you...," began Ellie finally, and when she saw her husband was waiting for her to finish the sentence, in spite of her embarrassment said, "taken me as your wife?"

He looked at her with a hopeless shrug. "You see, Elisabeth, I was so caught up in the harvest and the Princess and everything, that I didn't have... have *time* to think about it. I know I should have explained that. I was going to... do what you say, I swear, once we had mated the Princess and I knew everything there was all right."

Ellie looked at her husband, then burst out laughing, casting all modesty aside. "You mean, you couldn't think of mating with me because you were too busy thinking about who was going to mate with your Princess!"

"I'm not good at thinking about more than one thing at a time," he said apologetically. "And since we had a marriage of convenience, I thought we could do things when they were, well, convenient."

Ellie put her arms around his neck. "Oh, James! I think I should be insulted, but you know, I do understand. Only, do you think it will be convenient fairly soon, because I...," she blushed. "I want it to be."

He gave her his lovely smile. "It had damned well... sorry, it had better be convenient. Ever since I found your book about the odd boy I've been thinking of nothing else."

"Oh, I didn't mean for you to see that," said Ellie. "I don't know what made me do it. I think it was because I wanted to understand you. I do now, I think, I hope."

"But it was good I did see it, because the pictures were drawn so lovingly I knew you must be fond of me, a little," he said, holding her close.

"I've been more than fond of you for weeks," she confessed. "That's what made me say what I did. I've been wanting you to be a real husband for some time now. It was my hidden feelings coming out."

"What a fool I am! I wish you'd said something."

"If you'd ever tried to tell you something when your mind is fixed on something else, you'd understand," laughed Ellie. "You are absolutely single-minded, you just said it yourself! Anyway, a lady doesn't expect to have to persuade her own husband to… well, you know."

"You're right. I have been a poor excuse for a husband."

"No! You haven't. You've been kind and considerate. You had Mr. Fletcher take me around the estate, and arranged lunch with Mrs. Yeats. I found out you had the stables buy a new mild-tempered horse for the gig, especially for me. When I came to London on my own you arranged it all. The luncheon at the Red Lion and everything. I've never felt so looked-after in my life!" Then something occurred to her. "Why did you kiss me when I left? You'd never kissed me at all before. I wondered about that all the way to London."

"But you kissed me at the dinner table! I wondered about that, too. Nanny always kissed me goodbye like that. I think it was instinct."

"And there was I, thinking it meant something special!" laughed Ellie.

"Well, it did. As far as I know, Nanny never kissed anyone else. It was special. Anyway, let's make up for it now."

And he kissed her, not at all as Nanny used to kiss him.

They arrived back at Maylands just as the sun was setting. In fact, in later life, whenever she was away, that is how Ellie always thought of her home, bathed in a golden glow as if it had lit up specially for her. Relief showed plainly on Prewitt's face when she stepped out of the carriage on her husband's arm.

"I trust your mother is doing better?" he said.

"Oh, er…," she looked inquiringly at her husband.

"I explained to Prewitt that's why you left so abruptly," he said.

"Oh, yes, thank you Prewitt. It was a false alarm. Just something she had eaten, in fact."

As they walked upstairs to change for dinner, James said quietly, "It was really Prewitt who suggested that was the reason for you rushing off. But I understood it was a white lie, like you explained to me."

Ellie laughed. "I should hate to think I undid all Nanny's good work by teaching you to tell untruths!"

"But I trust you to tell me what to do, Ellie," replied her husband, looking at her seriously. "I'll always love Nanny but I don't think I need her in the same way now you are my wife."

Tears came to Ellie's eyes, but they were tears of joy.

Chapter Thirty-Four

Ellie's apartment was comfortably familiar, with its gently faded appearance and the rays of the dying sun throwing oblique patterns onto the old rugs. The five o'clock bell rang its familiar peal and Grace came in to help her change. The dresser asked if she had had a pleasant trip to London, and she was able to reply with sincerity that she had. It was comfortably familiar, too, to take a glass of Madeira in the drawing room with her husband, who sat next to her on the sofa, holding her hand and stretching his long legs in front of him.

"James," said his wife. " I think we should have a dinner for all our neighbors as soon as may be. I feel guilty at not inviting them before. I received cards from all sorts of people when I first got here, and didn't know how to reply."

"Ugh! Do we have to? I hate dinner parties!" Her husband looked dismayed.

"Yes, we do. You are the Marquess. As Sanderson would say, you have standards to maintain. Anyway, all you have to do is make inconsequential conversation."

"That's exactly what I hate and I'm no good at it."

"I'll teach you. It's easy. Let's begin. I'll pretend to be a lady guest. What chilly weather we've been having recently, my lord!"

He turned his dark gaze upon her. "Ellie! You know that's not true! The weather has been remarkably fine!"

"Oh, James! I'm just pretending! Imagine it had been wet and miserable. How would you respond to the lady?"

"I'd say: the wet weather seriously impacted the harvest. We were only able to get in half the hay before it got too wet to cut. It will be a disaster for the cattle over the winter. We may have to slaughter half of them."

Ellie laughed. "Oh, yes, that's just what a lady would like to talk about at the dinner table. Slaughtered cattle! You mustn't take everything so seriously!"

"But for a farmer a poor harvest is very serious!"

"I know, and so does everyone else who lives in the country. You have to acknowledge it has been bad but quickly change the subject. *'Yes, it has been very wet. It has made travelling about very difficult. I daresay you are looking forward to the spring. What plans do you have, Lady X?'*"

"Why should I care what plans she has?"

"You don't, of course, but it's always a good idea to get people talking about themselves. You'd be amazed how good a conversationalist you will be considered if you say nearly nothing but encourage others to talk. Try again. Well, my lord, what do you think of all the problems the Royal Family are having?"

"What the devil do I know or care about...," the Marquess protested, then collected himself, "Oh, I see." He thought for a moment. "It is sad. But I imagine many families have problems. What about yours Lady X? I hear your son has run off with the milkmaid."

"James! What on earth...!" She turned to him and saw he was grinning at her. Her dismay turned to laughter and she answered, "Yes, my lord. I'm afraid he has. That's the third in as many months. He's living with them all in a cottage on the estate and dresses himself in flowing robes. He says he is the reincarnation of an Eastern Potentate and these women are his harem."

"And he has ordered a gold carriage from the coachmakers, together with six white horses...," added the Marquess.

From there on they each added to the story of the unfortunate neighbor's son until they were both helpless with laughter and had to support each other into the breakfast room for dinner.

Cook had not known whether they would be back or not, and was able to put before them only a simple meal, as she termed it. There was a piece of pork, fresh from the farm that day, a loin of beef, leeks wrapped in bacon, several fillets of trout fried in butter, a dish of mashed swede, a compote of cherries, cabbage cooked with apples, and for the sweet course, a frangipane tart and a lemon pudding. James did justice to it all, declaring he was starving. He'd been made to survive on sandwiches for days, he said, grinning at her.

After dinner, Ellie fully expected her husband to go to see his Princess, but he astonished her by taking her arm and saying they would go for a walk. "As you pointed out, she's only a cow," he said. "She'll be there tomorrow. Anyway, if I'm in competition with a turnip, the turnip always wins."

After their walk, which was punctuated by kisses in the shadows that left Ellie breathless, they went upstairs.

"Tomorrow," said the Marquess, "I shall move into the bedchamber next to you. Tonight I shall sleep in your bed."

"Yes, my lord," said the Marchioness, her heart thumping.

As she prepared for bed, she thought nervously about the sight she had seen in front of the stables that day. Ellie wondered if her husband would have had any experience of what was required of him, and even more, whether she would know what was required of her.

She need not have worried. James was a kind and considerate lover, and she found that what her mother had said was right. It was all quite natural.

"I was worried neither of us would know what to do," she confided to her husband some days later.

"Why?" answered James, propping himself on an elbow and looking at her. "Did you think I had been living like a monk? What do you think my father took me to Paris for?"

"I thought it was for the pink biscuits."

Her husband laughed. "They were what I liked second best. And as for the thing I enjoyed the most, I've been reliably informed by persons who have considerable experience in these matters that I'm a natural. It must be those years of self-control."

"Another thing to thank Nanny for, then," said Ellie.

"Yes. Do you think I should tell her?"

"Of course not! She'd be horribly embarrassed. Oh!" Ellie was outraged until she saw her husband was grinning at her. "You know, I'm beginning to think I liked you better when you told the strict truth," she said.

"Too late," replied the odd Marquess, gathering his wife into his arms.

Epilogue

The Marquess and Marchioness of Hastings did give a number of successful dinner parties every year, and both became known as wonderful hosts. The Marquess, in particular, was much appreciated for his keen interest in his neighbors. Elisabeth continued to produce children's books, and, as generally happens, her notoriety receded. Sales increased, though, as people bought the books not because they were written by a notorious Lady, but for the charming illustrations and gently humorous stories. Her *Life in the Country* went into several editions. One book she never published was the *Life of an Odd Boy.* She did, however, finish the last page, but not until a year or so later.

Mr. Forsythe continued as typesetter for Woolstone & Browne, and fortunately soon met a young woman whom he was able to rescue from the unfortunate situation of an unhappy home life. She thought him a perfect knight in shining armor. He became a partner in the firm and ultimately sole proprietor. In time, Mr. Woolstone became as distant a memory as Mr. Browne. But by that time, thanks in large part to the Marchioness's books, the publishers were so well established with the old name, Mr. Forsythe thought it bad business to change it.

Ellie finished the new illustration of the Princess but it did not go into the book. James had it framed and hung in the portrait gallery, for, as he said, the heifer was an important part of family history. She had brought them together. In spite of James' horror at her unworthy mate, the Princess's first calf was a good sized animal, and subsequent offspring each outdid the other for weight and the ability to eat turnips.

To give his wife somewhere to read her stories to the children of the estate, James had a special cottage built. It had only one room inside, warmed by two good fireplaces. It was at first only used in the winter, as her ladyship always preferred to sketch and read outside. Later, when Ellie's life became too encumbered with other responsibilities, a teacher was taken on, and the place became a regular school.

The lad who so wanted to sleep in a hammock while sailing the seas was the fifth of five boys and felt his family could well do without him. He ran away to sea and by dint of hard work and careful husbandry, became captain of his own vessel. After some years, he sold it and went to Tahiti where he took several of the local women as wives. He lounged in the shade of the fruiting trees wearing a many-colored cloth skirt, just as he had first seen in her ladyship's book all those years before. He still had the book and showed it to his numerous offspring. Nothing in it surprised them, of course, as the people looked just as they looked themselves, but they were brought up to respect their father and always thanked him politely.

The Marquess's cousin was thwarted in his ambition to inherit Maylands when, a little over a year after their wedding, the Marchioness presented her proud husband with a healthy baby boy. It was then she illustrated the last page of her *Odd Boy* book. Her drawing was based on the portrait in the gallery depicting her husband as a baby with his mother, but this one featured three people.

It shows a brown-haired mama, sitting with her husband behind her, a protective hand on her shoulder, and the baby in her lap. Father and son have the same intent black gaze fixed on something only they can see. The Marchioness is smiling broadly.

The End

Excerpt from the best-selling Regency novel:
A Marriage is Arranged

"Listen to what I'm saying, Gareth," said the older lady, her silver blond hair covered by a very becoming lace bonnet.

"I am listening, Gran," said Gareth Wandsworth, fourth Earl of Shrewsbury, sitting uncomfortably in a chair in his grandmother's elegant drawing room, his powerful legs thrust out in front of him, his heavy eyebrows pulled together in a frown, "just as I've listened to you on this subject often before. It's not that I don't want to marry, it's just that I can't find a woman I can bear to face at the breakfast table for the next fifty years!"

"I've told you before! Do not call me by that low name! And you mean not one of them can bear the idea of facing *you* over the breakfast table!" replied his granddam tartly. "If your grandfather hadn't been so idiotic as to die when he did, there might have been some hope for you. You've never been what anyone could call good-looking, but when you became the Earl every girl of marriageable age buzzed around you like a bee to a honeypot. Your response was to get on your high horse and glower at them, so it's no surprise they all backed away.

"Then your addiction to the low sport of boxing has made your shoulders too... too *large*. You look positively frightening! What a pity you didn't take up fencing! That's the sport for a gentleman! I said at the time you were far too young to be in control of your fortune. I suppose you couldn't help being the next Earl, but it's a pity you didn't learn to be a little more conciliating."

"But Gran...."

"Do NOT call me that! And you know perfectly well what I mean! I hear nothing of you but your association with That Woman and

She Will Not Do! We need an heir produced by an acceptable woman. You surely don't want the title to go to Percy and his bloodless offspring."

Her grandson had a vision of his second cousin, a weak-willed individual whose slack, doughy body was sign enough of his lack of resolve. He had been snapped up by a sharp-faced woman a few years older than he. It was she who ruled both him and her timid son. If he inherited, it would be his wife who became Earl in all but name.

"Oh God." he muttered, "Anyone but Percy, or should I say Alicia?"

"Precisely. Find a sensible, well-bred young woman to be the mother of your sons, not Diane Courtland!"

"You know perfectly well I have no intention of marrying Diane, but I don't think any woman, well-bred or otherwise, could *guarantee* me sons," he retorted. Then he sighed. "The trouble is, the sensible, well-bred ones are all so dull! I swear I can hardly stay awake when I hear, *just so, my lord, of course, you are right my lord*, or, by way of a change, *I really couldn't say, my lord*. Doesn't a single one of them have an opinion on anything?"

"Of course not," replied his grandmother smartly. "They are not bred to have any opinion other than their father's and then their husband's. Besides, you alarm them too much with that scowl of yours. You have to find a woman who's not afraid of you."

But his lordship was tired of the same discussion they'd had many times before. "Look," he said, "if you really want me to marry one of this year's crop, put their names in a hat and pick one out. It's all the same to me. They are all equally lovely, equally accomplished, equally well-bred, and equally a dead bore. I promise I'll try not to frighten her."

"Don't be ridiculous! And if that's the way you feel about it, you may as well marry the girl your Papa pledged you to when she was born."

"What girl? What pledge?" The Earl sat up straight for the first time and looked at her intently. "This is the first I've heard about it!"

"I knew nothing of it either until I received a letter from the girl's mother the other day. That's why I asked you to come and see me."

She drew in her breath. "This is how it was. Your papa had a very good friend at Oxford, a Peter Grey. I remember him well. He came here often. A very pleasant, good-looking young man. In fact, your papa's chief objection to going to manage the family tea business in China was that that they wouldn't be able to run around together as they had been used to. But your grandfather needed him to go, and off he went.

"As you know, he came back to marry your mama, then returned to China, where you were born. What Peter Grey and he said to each other on that occasion I don't know, but when Grey subsequently married and his wife gave birth to a girl, they apparently exchanged letters agreeing that the two of you would be married. You were about seven at the time. It was just before you came home to go to Eton."

She stopped for a moment and put her lace handkerchief to her eyes. "But then, of course, your poor papa and mama were killed in that terrible way. We never knew the story, but it was something about payments and money. I could never forgive your grandfather for sending them there! Thank God you were already here! You would probably have perished too."

She was silent for a moment, lost in her memories, then continued. "Anyway, Grey's wife wrote to me quite recently to say her husband had passed away and telling me about the old promise. She has your Papa's letters agreeing to the match. The girl is eighteen now, but they couldn't bring her out while they were in black gloves and now they'll have to wait till the next season. In any case, it seems she's been away somewhere at school and cares nothing for society. According to her mama, she's very quiet and ladylike."

"Sounds perfect," said the Earl ironically. "Another dead bore. But she can't be any worse than the rest. Though," he said, as another idea struck him, "she may be a good deal better. If she cares nothing for society she won't mind staying at home building the nest while I go my own way, and if she's as well-bred as you think, she won't subject me to any scenes. I'll go to see her, and so long as she's passable, she may as well be the one."

He kissed his grandmother on the cheek and strode towards the door.

"If she'll have you, you mean," said his grandmother. But he was gone……..

To find out what happens to Gareth and his proposed bride, please go to:

https://www.amazon.com/Marriage-Arranged-Regency-Romance-ebook/dp/B0BS78MRCF

Note from the Author

Independent authors are very dependent on reader reviews. If you enjoyed this novel, please leave a review! Go to my Amazon page: www.amazon.com/GL-Robinson, and click on the title of the novel. Or use the QR code below. It will take you to the novel page. Scroll down to the Review area.

Thank you so much!

For a free short story and to listen to me read the first chapter of all my novels, please go to my website, or hover your phone camera over the QR code below.

https://romancenovelsbyglrobinson.com

Regency Novels by GL Robinson

Imogen or Love and Money. Lovely young widow Imogen is pursued by Lord Ivo, a well-known rake. She angrily rejects him and concentrates on continuing her late husband's business enterprises. But will she find that money is more important than love?

Cecilia or Too Tall to Love. Orphaned Cecilia, too tall and too outspoken for acceptance by the *ton,* is determined to open a school for girls in London's East End slums, but is lacking funds. When Lord Tommy Allenby offers her a way out, will she get more than she bargained for?

Rosemary or Too Clever to Love. Governess Rosemary is forced to move with her pupil, the romantically-minded Marianne, to live with the girl's guardian, a strict gentleman with old fashioned ideas about young women should behave. Can she save the one from her own folly and persuade the other that she isn't just a not-so-pretty face?

The Earl and The Mud-Covered Maiden. The House of Hale Book One. When a handsome stranger covers her in mud driving too fast and then lies about his name, little does Sophy know her world is about to change for ever.

The Earl and His Lady. The House of Hale Book Two. Sophy and Lysander are married, but she is unused to London society and he's very proud of his family name. It's a rocky beginning for both of them.

The Earl and The Heir. The House of Hale Book Three. The Hale family has a new heir, in the shape of Sylvester, a handful of a little boy with a lively curiosity. His mother is curious too, about her husband's past. They both get themselves in a lot of trouble.

The Kissing Ball. A collection of Regency short stories, not just for Christmas. All sorts of seasons and reasons!

The Lord and the Red-Headed Hornet. Orphaned Amelia talks her way into a man's job as secretary to a member of the aristocracy. She's looking for a post in the Diplomatic Service for her twin brother. But he wants to join the army. And her boss goes missing on the day he is supposed to show up for a wager. Can feisty Amelia save them both?

The Lord and the Cat's Meow. A love tangle between a Lord, a retired Colonel, a lovely debutante and a fierce animal rights activist. But Horace the cat knows what he wants. He sorts it out.

About The Author

GL Robinson is a retired French professor who took to writing Regency Romances in 2018. She dedicates all her books to her sister, who died unexpectedly that year and who, like her, had a lifelong love of the genre. She remembers the two of them reading Georgette Heyer after lights out under the covers in their convent boarding school and giggling together in delicious complicity.

Brought up in the south of England, she has spent the last forty years in upstate New York with her American husband. She likes gardening, talking with her grandchildren and sitting by the fire. She still reads Georgette Heyer.